Rohit Khilnani is the Entertainment Editor at Headlines Today. He specialises in Bollywood and has worked closely with the who's who of the Hindi film industry.

He started his career as a freelance writer for India's leading newspapers, including *The Times of India* and *Indian Express*. He has previously worked for NDTV and CNN-IBN. He follows the box-office and does the requisite number crunching every week. This book comes after he has completed 15 years of film reporting. He knows about film stars and their whereabouts like the back of his hand!

Rohit lives in Mumbai with his wife Yogita and his mother. He starts and ends his day by taking his dog, Pepper, for walks.

This is his first book, inspired in parts by real-life incidents.

I HATE BOLLYWOOD

Journey of Reporter Raghu

Rohit Khilnani

OM

Om Books International

Published in 2015 by

OM

Om Books International

Corporate & Editorial Office
A-12, Sector 64, Noida 201 301
Uttar Pradesh, India
Phone: +91 120 477 4100
Email: editorial@ombooks.com
Website: www.ombooksinternational.com

Sales Office
107, Ansari Road, Darya Ganj,
New Delhi 110 002, India
Phone: +91 11 2326 3363, 2326 5303, 4000 9000
Fax: +91 11 2327 8091
Email: sales@ombooks.com
Website: www.ombooks.com

ISBN: 978-93-83202-13-3

Printed in India

10 9 8 7 6 5 4 3 2 1

For Mamma

Contents

1

My Bollywood Debut

I, Raghu Kumar, was born and brought up in a middle-class family in Chembur, Mumbai; a suburb that was dominated by the film industry in the '70s and the '80s. I had grown up watching the popular celebrities who lived here—veteran Ashok Kumar, brothers Anil and Boney Kapoor, Om Prakash, Shilpa Shetty, Malaika Arora and Vidya Balan. Those who didn't live here were spotted at the RK Studios in Chembur.

Playing outdoor in the evenings meant running into Bollywood actors, like Anil Kapoor, who was already established in the '80s. It also meant getting scolded by the veteran Hindi film actor, Ashok Kumar, if your cricket ball hit his window. Almost every time our cricket ball landed in his compound or hit his window pane we just had to go and buy another ball or call it a day. He was kind to us most of the times but he hated being disturbed when he was sitting in his compound in the evening. Some of the boys used to deliberately throw a ball in the garden to get a glimpse of the veteran actor. There were days when he would come out and meet us, shake hands and sign autographs; with that he ensured his loyal fans in the neighbourhood were happy. When we used to go back home and tell our parents that Ashok uncle scolded us because the cricket ball hit his window, each of us would get a scolding from our respective parents.

The words almost always were, 'You should not do that again. He is a very senior actor and you should respect him. Don't play near his house, play somewhere else.'

I never understood why our parents sided with him all the time, but that didn't stop us from playing near his garden. We were way too young to understand how he had won the hearts of an entire generation.

When I used to hang around with the high school boys, they would always talk about the hottie Malaika Arora, who lived in a rented apartment in our colony. She was sexy even then, but not as popular; her career as a veejay took off much later. She was used to being gawked at, by youngsters in the neighbourhood, each time she stepped out.

My mom knew the popular film producer Boney Kapoor and his actor brother Anil very well. I clearly remember a few interactions with them. All they did was pull my cheeks and I hated it every time.

Each time they met my mom and me they would say, '*Arre kitna bada ho gaya hai* Raghu! (Raghu has grown up so much!)' Then they would look at me and ask, 'Actor *banega?* (Do you want to become an actor?)'

We had another neighbour, Alok Kapoor, who was a film producer, albeit not a very successful one. He was tall, had a deep voice and an impressive personality. My mom told me that his name was Alok Rao, but when he started making movies he changed it to Alok Kapoor. It didn't make any sense to me, till years later when I discovered that film folks believe that the surname Kapoor or Kumar always ensured popularity.

One summer morning, Alok uncle came over to our house. He asked my mom if my elder sister, Reena, could do a role, as a child artiste, in his next film *Mahajwala*. It was the year 1987 and Reena was in the sixth standard while I was in my fourth. Being a single parent, my mom wanted both her kids to experiment life as it came and since summer vacations were on, she gave a go ahead to Alok Kapoor. I was very upset because I too wanted to act in the film, especially as I thought I had the looks. But I was told by Alok uncle that he will take me in his next film.

'*Beta, Alok Kapoor ka waada*. (Son, its Alok Kapoor's promise.)'

I really didn't know what that meant and I didn't care whose promise it was. I was hell bent on acting in *Mahajwala*. My sister and I had a lot of fights because of this as she was not one to mince words.

'Raghu, now deal with it. I have a role and you don't. If you had the looks you would get a role too!'

I cried and went to mom. She scolded Reena. This was the usual practice, the younger sibling cries and the elder one gets scolded and I obviously took advantage of it. I thought I was fairly decent looking. I was thin; definitely not obese like most of the boys in my class. I always dressed well, had light brown eyes and dark brown hair. Hence I failed to understand why I was not offered a role in the film.

Some outdoor shoots were scheduled for *Mahajwala* in Leh, Jammu and Kashmir. I was also a part of Reena's entourage by default; my mom had to be with Reena and I couldn't be left alone in Mumbai. The producer took care of all the expenses and my mom took permission from our tuition teachers. They too were excited and assured my mom that they would cover up the syllabus by taking some extra classes for us once we were back. Even though holidays were on, mom thought it was necessary to inform the school Principal, Father Paul, who was a very kind man.

'So the new breed of actors is in our school. I am proud of Reena already. Please make sure once they are back and school starts, they concentrate on studies and not think about the shooting,' Father Paul said with a smile.

My mom used to make both Reena and me touch Father Paul's feet everytime we visited him. He used to give us a rose everytime we left his office. Reena used to be happy, but for boys, roses didn't make sense at that age.

We travelled to Jammu by train in the first class compartment. The entire trip and all the meals were paid by the film crew. As kids, both of us were pampered. Two compartments were booked for the film team. The production team made sure we were well looked after—at every station they would get us hot *chai* and some times *chaat*.

Once we were in Kashmir, my sister would wake up early, get ready and go to shoot her scenes and I used to wake up only around 10 a.m. and order room service. I was having the time of my life! After breakfast I would laze in bed and watch TV as long as I wanted. These were things I had never done before. In fact, I had never travelled out of Mumbai or stayed in a hotel. Once I was ready, a unit car would drop me to the shooting location.

One day when I reached the site I saw Alok uncle looking tensed. The shoot was getting delayed. I asked the spotboy, 'What happened?'

He informed that for a scene the director needed some beggars in the background but we could not find any Kashmiri locals for this. Alok uncle stared at me for a few minutes and realised that I would fit the role perfectly. He went to my mom and asked her if he could use me in the background, as a beggar. He used the word, 'background artist.'

Even before I knew what I had to do, I jumped with joy, 'Mom please, please, I want to be in the background. All my school friends will see me and it will be so nice. Please, please, say yes.'

Left with little choice my mom agreed, on the condition that my face wouldn't be seen. I knew that... but at least I could tell my friends that I acted in the film and it was not just my sister's film.

Alok Kapoor needed me, I had certainly arrived! I had been offered a role. Yes, this is what I was going to tell all my friends—that I had been offered a role.

The scene was pretty simple. I had to turn my back to the camera and when the director called out 'action,' a couple sitting on a bench under a tree would throw a *roti* from their plate. I had to jump and catch the *roti* before it touched the ground. Basically my fielding talent was going to be tested! I was given torn clothes and my hair was messed up. Nothing had to be done to my face because I didn't have to face the camera.

In about three takes Alok uncle said, 'Okay. Got it.'

I was the happiest person on the set. The scene was supposed to be a part of the montage where the film shows poverty. I couldn't wait to get back, to tell all my friends that I was an actor. My sister laughed at me through the whole episode but I couldn't care less because I was part of the film. It was a landmark moment for me! My mom was happy only because I had stopped crying and troubling her about wanting to act in the film.

When we returned to Mumbai, I told all my friends and teachers, in school that I had acted in a film and would let them know when the film was released.

The reactions made me smile and feel important, 'Wow buddy! What is your role in it? When will the film release?'

While *Mahajwala* was being shot, Boney uncle released his film, *Mr India*, that went onto become a blockbuster. The film had a lot of child actors and was extremely popular with school kids. I remember we were invited for the premiere of the film and Boney uncle welcomed us with a broad smile.

After shooting that one scene for *Mahajwala* I started daydreaming. I believed that after my film *Mahajwala* released I would be as popular as all the kids from *Mr India*. The day finally came and *Mahajwala* was released. My family, my cousins and friends were very excited but I couldn't understand why it didn't have the buzz that *Mr India* had at the time of release. Why was no one talking about *Mahajwala* in school? Why was there no premiere? My mom told me that Alok uncle had put all his money in this film and there was no money for a premiere. His future as a director depended on *Mahajwala* becoming a success.

On the day of the release, my mom was given about 20 tickets of Basant Cinema in Chembur, for family and friends. It was for the night show. The air conditioning wasn't working and though the fans were on, it was suffocating inside. The film started with my sister's sob story and she was there through the first 10 minutes of the film. That's about it. Everyone told her that she had acted very well. I was waiting for my scene, which I had done with all my heart, but the scene was not there in the film!

I asked my mom softly, 'What happened? How is my scene not there?'

Even she didn't know why my scene had been cut. She was anyway surprised that with all the shooting that she had done, my sister would be there onscreen only for the first 10 minutes. But at least my cousins had registered my sister's presence onscreen. What about me? What was I going to tell all my friends? They were going to laugh at me.

I was angry, 'Why didn't Alok uncle tell me that he was chopping my only scene? Why did he shoot it in the first place?' I had so many questions, not to mention the task of facing my friends and cousins who knew that I was in the film. I came home and cried till I could cry no more. My mom convinced me that she would tell Alok uncle to take me in his next film.

I was however far from being convinced. I cried all the more, 'I don't want to hear Alok uncle's name ever again. I hate Alok uncle, I hate Bollywood!'

She put me to sleep by telling me that she would tell Boney uncle to take me in his next film. *Mahajwala* bombed at the box-office and no one saw Alok uncle after that. Mom said he had to sell his house to return the money he had borrowed to make the film. Apparently, he moved to Nepal; he had fled the city because he owed money to a lot of people. We never heard of him again. That was my introduction to the movie business.

2

Friendship and Betrayal

All of us have had our share of good friends and best friends when we were young. My best friend was Vijay Kapoor who came from a popular Bollywood family. We were in the same class, always with consecutive roll numbers and scored pretty much the same marks every year and we were inseparable. The only difference was that he came from a rich and famous '*filmy*' family whereas I came from a middle-class family.

Everyone spoke about our friendship; we were the *Jai* and *Veeru* of our area. My family and friends were very happy when Vijay came to my house. I never saw him as an actor's son; to me he was like any one of us. The only thing that was special was that he was my closest friend. He was a good-looking boy and everyone knew he would grow up to be an actor. My cousins always asked him questions about his father Amit Kapoor who was a superstar. His mom Maya Kapoor had also been an actress before her marriage.

Vijay always had the coolest things; his pencil box, water bottle, tiffin box, crayons and even his school bag was from the US. His dad used to get him lot of gifts each time he visited the US for shoots. Vijay also travelled with him several times, and showed us pictures of him with other film stars. Meeting film actors however was no big deal for Vijay. Even I visited RK Studios many times when Vijay's father was shooting. I also got to see his dad's co-stars who were shooting with him on the same sets. Thanks to Vijay, my autograph book was full of autographs of the who's who of Bollywood; some I took myself when I met the stars at RK Studios while the others Vijay got for me when he met the other actors.

Everytime Vijay wanted to come to my place, his driver dropped him in his Mercedes and picked him up at a specified time. The driver never let Vijay hold his school bag or carry anything; he also opened the car door for him. While boys like me longed to sit in a car, Vijay was driven around the city in a huge Mercedes. We loved everything that he had and he loved the little things that I had. He loved the food that my mom cooked and loved just being at my place. His parents were always travelling; hence, he spent a lot of time at my place because he did not want to be at home, alone, inspite of half a dozen servants. Most of the time, his maids woke him up, dressed him and sent him to school and he was back home to them.

Soon after school, where we spent a lot of time together, he would reach home and call me on my landline, 'Raghu what are you doing? I am getting bored. Can I come over to your house?'

'I am taking a nap so come in the evening,' I would reply. At my place, afternoon was only meant for naps.

Even when Vijay's parents were in Mumbai they were too busy to spend time with him. I was not just his friend, I was his family.

For some odd reason Vijay often asked, 'Raghu, you are my best friend. What will happen if we are not friends some day?'

'Why will we not be friends?' I wondered at his strange question.

My mom didn't like me going out with Vijay's family. This was after an incident when Amit Kapoor got drunk and insulted me at a club in front of a lot of people. It happened some time ago.

Vijay used to go with his family to the Big Splash Club in New Bombay, every Sunday morning. He would always insist that I join him. I could not avoid when he really insisted.

That day after the swim all of us changed and got ready for lunch. By then Amit uncle was already a few drinks down. His post-drinking brawls and drama were common occurrences. We were all sitting on a long table by the pool. Vijay's family friends and cousins had also come that day.

Amit uncle looked at me and said, 'Where did your mom buy this shirt from? Linking road?' He then laughed loudly!

Vijay's mom tried to tell him to stop and no one at the table found it funny except him. I felt insulted but kept quiet and continued eating. He held out a bottle of Black Label at me and asked, 'Want to drink?'

Everyone told him to stop bullying me but he wouldn't listen.

'*Itni mehengi* whiskey *hai; shaayad tujhe phir dekhne ko bhi na mile*!' he mocked, asking me to take a swig as I might not get the opportunity to taste this expensive whiskey again.

He got up and came towards me with the bottle, insisting that I have one sip. His brother and his wife got up and stopped him. As he approached, fear and humiliation made my tears flow. I was seething inside. I wanted to go back home. Vijay also felt bad but didn't know what to say.

I came home and told my mom everything and she was very angry. She called Vijay's mom, who apologised profusely. That day my mom decided that I would never go out with them again.

Reena was angry, 'When Vijay comes to our house I will also insult him. He should know what it feels like to be humiliated.'

'No! We don't do that to our guests, Reena. That's not how you were brought up, right?'

'Yes, but what they did to Raghu is so mean mom! They do this because we don't have a father.'

Mom never let us feel the absence of a father, but incidents like these pinched and made Reena feel that we were bullied as a family, by a lot of people, only because of the absence of a male head of the family.

'Reena! I am your father. I picked up the phone and made Vijay's mom realise that the mistake was totally Amit's…didn't I?'

'Yes mom! I'm sorry!'

Mom hugged Reena.

She told me if Vijay wanted to play with me he was most welcome to our house but I would never go to his place or go out with his family ever again.

Hence, Vijay started spending a lot of time at my place. So, each time Vijay's parents called to check on him he was never home because he was always at my place. It started troubling them and soon they stopped him from coming over to my place by instructing the servants to not allow him out of the house and the driver to not drop him at our place. Vijay called me and told me this.

'What's your dad's problem?' I asked.

'I don't know, but he said that I should not go over to your place very often.'

'That's weird, isn't it? They are never home anyway, so how does it matter if you spend the evening at my place?'

Vijay didn't have an answer.

I told my mom what Amit Kapoor had told his son, my best friend. She also found it absurd but said that she didn't expect any better from him. 'Raghu, if his dad wants him to stay away from you, then you should stay away from him,' she said.

'No he didn't say that, mom! He said not to visit our house often.' I defended him because I wanted Vijay to come over often.

'Yes, today he has said this and tomorrow he will say, "Don't visit their house at all." Raghu, you should know that film actors are unreasonable. They don't think like us.'

'*Us*? How are we different?'

'They are very rich and famous. We are not. We are normal people who live normal lives.'

'But Vijay is normal mom. You know that. Right?'

'Vijay is young now. He will grow up the way his father wants him to. Or let me correct and say this, he will *have to* grow up the way his father wants him to. His choices will actually be the choices made by his dad.'

I was very hurt because deep-down I knew what my mom was saying was true but I was too close to Vijay to think of parting ways. At the age of 14 it is not easy to digest the possibility that your best friend of four years might decide to end the friendship.

I did not have to wait long for my mom's prediction to come true. Vijay suddenly stopped calling me and coming to my place. I tried calling him a couple of times and learnt that he had left for America with his dad. Later when I called, his maid told me that he was playing in the garden with his friends. I knew that was a lie because Vijay didn't have any friends, apart from me. Finally, when Vijay came back to school, he ignored me completely and even started walking in the opposite direction.

I caught him in the class before our teacher came in.

'What's wrong? Why don't you return my calls?'

'Nothing, Raghu. We can't be friends anymore and I won't be coming to your house now.'

'But why? What happened? What did I do? You can't do this Vijay! We are best friends.'

'I got a bad beating from my dad a few days ago. Even my mom didn't come to my rescue.'

'But why did he hit you? What did he say?'

'He said I should not go to anyone's house like that. I have a lot of responsibility because we are a famous family and that you are my friend only because of my background. You get to meet actors because of me. He said that people would use me all my life, so I have to be careful.'

'And you believe your dad? Come on Vijay! I am your friend because we get along well. It has nothing to do with your father or your mom.'

He looked down, avoiding my eyes, and said, 'I don't have a choice Raghu!'

'What did your mom say? She knows me well! Didn't she tell your father that he is wrong?'

'Mom just said whatever Dad was saying was right. I was too young to understand all this and had to listen to him or I would be sent to the boarding school.'

The teacher walked in then and our conversation was cut short. It was pretty much over anyway! The decision had been taken and I had been told that my best friend was not even a friend anymore.

Vijay didn't talk to me during the break and not even after school and never again after that day. There were boys from other Bollywood families in our school and Vijay started hanging out with them. I was left with no one. I had not bothered to make other friends because Vijay filled up my life and I didn't need anyone else. He moved on faster than I could have ever imagined.

Seeing me upset about the whole episode, mom told me to make friends with people like *us*—normal people. Not sons of film stars.

3

Journalism Beckons

Reena was a pretty girl. She was way too stylish and always ahead of her times when it came to fashion trends. Styling came naturally to her and she took that up professionally as well. She had a lot of friends in the fashion industry and she soon became an assistant stylist with a top designer lable. I grew up to be a decent-looking boy but I made sure that after the unhappy episode with Vijay Kapoor, I didn't make any friends with people related to Bollywood. In college I had a lot of friends, all normal non-*filmi* people. Life was less complicated with them. I was good with numbers and I had a flair for writing. While I was in college I wrote the editorials for the annual college magazine. My contribution would always be the cover story, usually an interview with some successful alumni. That is the reason the strict principal was always nice to me even when I was caught bunking lectures.

She always returned my I-card with, 'Don't do this Raghu, you are a nice boy.'

I was let off each time while my friends had to call their parents and get humiliated in front of them by the staff members. There were times when the principal was extremely rude to them. I hated it when she did that to my friends. I wished I could write about it in the college magazine, but obviously I couldn't and since she was nice to me there was no way I could afford to upset her.

Through common friends I was introduced to some journalists in my last year of college and they gave me local assignments which I did after college; assignments like covering events at clubs and the Gymkhana lawns, small feature stories, inauguration of flyovers and new stores and other stories regarding the city.

An editor once told me, 'Raghu, the reason I like giving you work is because you never say no to any story. Keep this attitude always and do all stories that come your way; big or small. That's what journalists are supposed to do.'

I was always good at networking and I made a lot of contacts while I was freelancing for different magazines and newspapers. By the time I finished college I had written for the Mumbai editions of all the leading newspapers in the country.

Now I wanted a full-time job. The popular journalists in those days were all children of well-known journalists or relatives of some other influential people.

My mom knew a gentleman named Mahesh Ramchandani in our colony. He used to borrow books from her. I discovered that he was a senior journalist and asked my mom to put in a word for me. She decided to take me to his place to officially introduce me to him, with the hope that he would help me if he knew of any job opportunity.

When we reached his house, he was sitting in his garden, sipping tea and reading a book. He saw us, kept his book on the table and walked up to greet us at the gate. His white Labrador came running after him.

'Hi! Come, come. Are you scared of dogs? Then I will put him inside.'

'Not at all. I love dogs. What's his name?' I asked.

'He is Simba, usually very lazy but when he sees new people he will come to sniff and hang around; to show that he is an alert dog. But the fact is that he is a lazy bum.

'How have you been Aunty?' He asked my mom.

'I am good.'

'Tell me, how can I help you?'

'Raghu, my son, has been writing for a while. He is a freelance journalist...and...'

He interrupted her, 'I am aware of that Aunty. I have read his bylines. He is doing some interesting stories.' He then looked at me and continued, 'The other day you did a story on the traffic problem near Chembur station, right?'

My smile broadened. 'Yes!' It felt great when someone said that to me. The idea of people reading your work is the best compliment possible for a journalist or an author.

'That was a much-needed story. The Chembur station is a mess. Hope some authorites read your story and do something about it.'

Mom continued, 'So now that his college is over. I thought if you could guide him on how he should go about looking for a job in a newspaper...'

'Of course! I don't work with any publication right now. I am busy writing a book. But I will give you some references of friends who are still in the media. It may take time because getting a job with a newspaper is not easy, so have patience. And I am only going to give you references, which means I will tell you who to meet and cannot guarantee you a job.'

'Sure. That will be fine.' I wondered how that would help but I also knew that sending resumes to email IDs and post boxes wouldn't help. So he was actually doing me a huge favour.

He continued, 'Go and meet Rajeev Mehra. He is a senior film journalist with *The News*. Give him my reference and then let me know what he says. Till then I will dig out some other contacts for you.'

I got the address of *The News* and visited their office in the narrow lanes of Dadar flower market the very next day. Since this was my first interaction for a job, I was dressed in formals. I carried a file which had my resume and some of my recently published articles. I reached the reception and asked for Rajeev Mehra. There was no receptionist, just a peon segregating the press releases from the piles of other papers.

He looked up for half a second and continued his work, '*Kisse milna hai?* PRO *hai tum?* Press release *box mein daalo aur jaao.* (Who do you want to meet? Are you a PRO? If you want to drop a press release, drop it in the box and leave.)'

I was quick to respond, '*Nahi nahi.* Rajeev Mehra *se milna hai. Unke dost ne bheja hai! Mai* freelance journalist *hoon.* (No, no. I want to meet Rajeev Mehra. His friend has asked me to meet him. I am a freelance journalist.)'

'*Arre itna subah kaun aata hai. Jaao barah baje ke baad aana.* (No one comes so early. Go now and come after 12 p.m.)'

He didn't even look at me while he was talking, just continued with the work at hand.

I stepped out and walked in the bylanes of the Dadar flower market. The smell of fresh flowers in the air was refreshing. I thought I would buy some for my mom if I got the job. I stopped at a tea stall to have some hot tea and kill time. A group of photographers was also present with their respective camera bags. I realised that they were from *The News* from the press cards hanging around their necks. They were cribbing about their jobs.

A plump photographer in the group was cribbing that he had been working with the company for two years now but his salary was really very little. He had even spoken to the bureau chief but to no avail.

It was not the best conversation to run into when you are looking forward to joining the same workplace.

I had some tea and walked towards Kabootar Khana since I had a lot of time to kill. I found walking into these old lanes of the real Mumbai very fascinating. People had come to feed the pigeons. Just watching them was therapeutic. Some of them were chanting prayers and feeding the pigeons for a long time while others just stopped for a few seconds, left the grains and rushed to work. I sat there just looking at the pigeons squabbling with each other for the grains, although there was enough for all. An old man sat nearby selling handkerchiefs. Since there were no buyers in the morning he was doing what I was doing—watching the pigeons.

I asked him, '*Yahan kafi log roz kabutaron ko khilane ke liye aate hai kya?* (Do many people come here everyday to feed these birds?)'

I was just expecting a yes or a no but he had a lot to say, '*Arre saab* India *mein koi bhooka nai marta hai. Jail mein bhi logon ko khaana milta hai aur peepal ke pedh ke neechi cheetiyon ko bhi log khana dete hain.* (Sir, in India no one goes hungry. Even if you are in jail you get food. People even feed ants staying under a *peepal* tree.)'

I didn't get the answer to my question but I didn't dare ask him again. Sometimes a polite 'hmmm' is the best way to end a conversation. It was 12:30 p.m. I got up and walked back to the newspaper office.

The peon saw me and said, '*Haan aa gaye* Rajeev Mehra *saab. Aage se* right. (Yes, Rajeev Mehra has come. Go straight ahead to your right.)'

He had a cubicle in a big newsroom which had a handful of people at that hour. I walked quietly towards him, hoping that he would not just dismiss me and my request.

'Hi, sir. I am Raghu Kumar. Mr Mahesh Ramchandani asked me to meet you. I am a freelance journalist.'

'Oh! Mahesh is a dear friend. Come, pull up a chair. I will call for some coffee.'

'No sir, actually I was here at 10 a.m. So I had a cup of tea outside.'

'I wish you had called before coming. I would have told you that we start only around noon. So, tell me what do you write about? What beat do you cover?'

'I don't have any specific beat yet. Since I am a freelancer, I cover whatever the newspaper asks me to, sometimes just events and inaugurations. Sometimes I do stories on education or even transport.'

'I am not sure if you are aware that I handle the film pages. So if that's something that interests you then I can check with the editor of the newspaper to find out if we are hiring.'

'I would definitely be interested. That would be really great.'

Rajeev gave me a reassuring nod, 'Okay, you leave your resume with me and I will get back to you soon.'

I handed him my documents and with the assurance that he would call me if there was an opening, I stepped out of his cubicle.

When I stepped out of the newsroom, I saw the peon walking in. '*Eh* freelancer! *Kaam hua? Mile* Rajeev Mehra *se?* (Hey freelancer! Did you get your work done? Met Rajeev Mehra?)'

I just smiled and left. I told myself if I get a job here, the first thing I would like to do is give this cocky man a piece of my mind.

The bus journey from Dadar to Chembur was fun because I kept dreaming about the job at *The News*—what I was going to wear to work, would I need a motorbike to travel as I would have to go out for stories, how it would be to flash my press card.

Once I got home, I realised that I was hungry. I could smell mom's homemade Chinese food. She always made it spicy and it smelt awesome. Exactly the way most Indians love Chinese food.

'Met Rajeev Mehra? How was it?' Mom asked me as I stepped inside the house.

'It was great. He is a very nice man. He is going to call in a day or two so please don't miss any phone calls.' I checked the volume of our white cordless phone. The volume button was at the maximum point, but I still pushed it up to ensure that the volume, for the incoming calls, would be at the highest. I also made sure the television ran on really low volume till I heard from Rajeev Mehra. I didn't want to take any chances.

Rajeev Mehra called the same evening. My mom came running with the cordless.

'Hi Raghu. Are you willing to work hard?' He asked pointedly.

I responded with a prompt *Yes*.

'You can come from tomorrow. I have spoken to the editor. You would be paid per article for the first few months and would be expected to contribute for the film pages, which come every Saturday.

I thanked him profusely and promised to reach work early the next day.

'You can come around noon.' I could sense the smile in his voice on the other side and remembered that the office had been practically empty till noon that morning.

There was an impromptu celebration at my place. I called all my cousins and told them that I would be writing for *The News*.

'Raghu, wake up early tomorrow. We will first go to the temple and then you start your work.' Mom told me when I was finally ready to hit the bed after all the celebrations.

At the temple, mom told pandit*ji* to put a *tikka* on my forehead which I promptly removed with my new white handkerchief on my way to work. Mom said that she would be visiting Mahesh with some *mithai* and I should also visit him after work to thank him.

She wanted to drop me off at the bus stop, but I said a firm no. I was after all taking my first step towards becoming completely independent today. It was my first day at my first job.

After a wait of 10 minutes, I got into BEST bus no. 90 which dropped me right outside the lane of my new office in Dadar. For a few minutes, I stood staring at the sign, *The News*, outside the office. I still couldn't believe that I would be working for *The News*.

I noticed the smug peon again; sitting at the same place with his specs on his nose, this time doing something with some fax papers.

'*Arre tum*...freelancer *na? Phir aa gaye? Kaam hua nai kya kal?* (You again? Aren't you the freelancer? Didn't you get your work done yesterday?)'

'*Kaam ho gaya, isiliye mai aaya hoon.* Reporter *hoon* Rajeev Mehra *kii* team *mein.* (I am here because I got my work done. I am now a reporter in Rajeev Mehra's team.)'

'*Arre wah! Peda kidhar hai? Mai Patil hoon, idhar kaa peon. Subah dus se barah baje main fax aur post check karta hoon. Uske baad kuch kaam ho to bolna. Aur kal peda chahiye humko.* (Wow! Where are the sweets? My name is Patil and I am the peon here. From 10 in the morning till noon, I check the fax and the post. After that if you have any work for me then let me know. And get sweets tomorrow.)'

'*Aur barah ke baad* reception *pe kaun baithta hai?* (Who sits at the reception after 12 p.m?)' I asked.

'*Koi nai. Aate jaate koi* office boy *baitha to baitha. Michelle kaam karti thi but pagaar kam hone ke wajah se woh chhodke chali gayi. Uske baad hum hi dekhte hain* reception *kaa kaam. Aisi baat nahi hai kii hamara paghar jiada hai but chalta hai, kaam to karna hai!* (No one. Sometimes some office boys sit here. Michelle was the receptionist but she quit because her salary was less. After that we only manage the reception. It's not that we get paid a lot of money but its okay. One has to work right!)'

Once inside the newsroom I felt awkward. I was standing in the huge office of a popular newspaper and I didn't know a soul apart from my boss Rajeev who I had met only briefly. What should I do? Where should I sit? I just waited near his desk.

Rajeev walked in after about half an hour, 'Why are you standing there? Sit here, this is your computer.'

It was a few desks away from where he sat.

He then introduced me to whoever was in sight. The usual early birds in office were Dey and Shradha, I was told, and they were the most helpful around here.

'Your surname is Kumar. You should become an actor. Why do you want to be a journalist and spoil your life?' Dey said. Since he was loud, everyone laughed at his joke, which I did not find amusing at all.

Rajeev Mehra also introduced me to the editor and the photographers. Since it was the first day, he asked me to just hang around and see how work got done here—how pages were made, what were the different deadlines for the different pages, and other details related to the newspaper.

'It's your first job so if you have any questions don't hesitate to ask. Give yourself a month and you will know exactly how a newspaper works,' Rajeev told me confidently.

During lunch time, I was asked to join the other reporters in the canteen. The lunch *thaali* was for Rs 2.50, but my mom had packed my *dabba*. Everyone pounced upon it. Most of the reporters were from different cities and I was told that they craved for home food. That's when I started valuing my *dabba* food a lot more.

Shradha, a senior colleague, said, 'These people will finish your *dabba* everyday and you have to eat this canteen *thali,* so I suggest you tell your mom to pack some extra food,' and added in a whisper, 'Lot of *bhukkar*s here.'

I was bored by the end of the day because I had nothing to do. Everyone else was typing something on their computers. I walked up to the newspaper stand; that's the place where all the daily newspapers were tied to an ugly rope.

I had noticed Patil walk in with the afternoon newspapers, make a hole at the top left hand corner with a screwdriver and tie each of the newspapers to the free end of the rope.

'What is the need to tie up the newspapers?' I had asked Patil.

'*Arre log ghar lekar jaate hain! Kya bolega*,' he responded, rolling his eyes in exasperation.

Did people really take the newspapers home, as Patil was suggesting, I wondered. I decided to ask Rajeev.

Rajeev laughed out aloud when I asked him, 'Who told you that?'

'Patil,' I responded.

'*Uff!* He is mad! Don't take him seriously. The idea is that the newspapers should be in one place, so that we know where to go when we have to refer to a recently published story. Else the newspapers will be scattered all over the newsroom. At the end of the day these newspapers go to the library where they are stored for two months or so, in case we need to refer to an old newspaper.'

'This makes sense. Patil is weird. Isn't he?'

'Good you figured that out so soon! We took a long time to crack that stupid nut.'

The photographer who I had overheard cribbing about his pay earlier walked up to me to introduce himself.

'Hi. I am Naresh, Senior Photographer. Looking forward to working with you.'

'Same here, Naresh.'

'I think I have seen you somewhere before.' Naresh looked at me with curious eyes.

'Yes you have. I was at the *chai* stall that day, when you were talking to your colleagues about the salary.'

Naresh looked embarrassed for a few seconds before breaking into a laugh. He said, 'Don't mention this to anybody,' and walked away with a guilty smile.

'Don't worry Naresh. I won't mention it to anyone.'

Newsrooms then were not the way they are now. The walls were off white and boring.When the AC didn't work, it was too hot because the fans were too high up. It didn't really make a difference even if they were switched on at full speed. There was internet connection only on one computer and everyone had to wait in a queue to check their mails. At that time most of us had only Yahoo and Hotmail accounts. There was no TV in the newsroom for reporters. There was only one in the editor's room, a place which I visited only once or twice throughout my tenure at *The News*.

I took the bus back home at the end of the day. Bus no. 90 took 45 minutes and dropped me right outside my house. My mom and sister were waiting to hear from me. I was tired as it was unusual to be out all day and then travel back all the way by bus. My family wanted to know all about my first day at work but I kept saying I had done nothing.

My sister, who had flexible timings, was always home when I was home. She repeatedly asked, 'But, you must have done something, *na*?'

'Yes, met everyone. Had lunch with them and everyone loved your food, mom.'

Thereafter, the good part now was that each time I was introduced to anyone socially, in my family or friends circle, I was introduced as a reporter from *The News*. This was the year 2000 and a reporting job had a lot of credibility. This was way before the 'Breaking News' culture started.

My first assignment was to interview actor Sunil Shetty; his name didn't have an extra 'e' in those days. I was told that he was one of the most down-to-earth actors around. I found that out for myself; even in the first meeting he was warm and forthcoming. I took down notes in my writing pad as he answered my questions. I didn't have a voice recorder, which made life a lot easier for print reporters.

I told Sunil Shetty that my family was very fond of him and he asked me to get my mom and sister next time I came to meet him.

When I returned to the office, Rajeev asked me, 'So, how was your first interview?'

'It was very good,' I responded eagerly.

'Yes, Sunil is a nice guy. You still have to meet some tough celebrities! File the story if you are not doing anything else. We will take it for the Saturday page tomorrow. Write around 400 words, not more.'

I couldn't wait to see my byline. I filed it and left for the day.

The same night Reena got a bad asthma attack and we had to take her to the hospital. We were awake till late into the night. Inspite of the anxiety, there was a sense of happy aniticipation at the back of my mind; I knew that the next morning I was going to see my first byline in *The News*.

The next morning, I was the first person to rush to the door for the newspaper; picking up the milk was just an eventuality I told myself as I handed the packet to my mom, who I noticed looked really tired after the ordeal of the previous evening.

I went through the newspaper, looking for my interview but couldn't find it. In fact, the film page was missing from the newspaper.

I called Rajeev at his residence landline. I had to also tell him that my sister was in the hospital. He had already left for work and so I had to wait for him to reach office. When I called him at work later, he agreed that I had to be with my family now and granted leave for two days.

'What happened to the film page today?' I asked him finally, voicing what had been bothering me.

'Oh yes! We needed to feature a full page ad. It happens. But don't worry, we will carry your interview next week,' Rajeev responded in a matter-of-fact way dismissing my disappointment at not seeing my article in the newspaper.

So I had to wait for a whole week to see my byline.

In the following week, the interview with Sunil Shetty finally appeared and then my stories and interviews were a regular feature on the film page every week. Actors knew about me—even those who had not met me.

I realised when I was introduced to them over several occasions. 'Oh! So you are Raghu Kumar! We read your stories,' most of them said. It was a great feeling. The idea of being known by your byline was an awesome achievement.

4

Where's the Party Tonight?

It's a myth that film journalists party with film stars. Stars party with their friends and we party with ours. They celebrate festivals with their family members and close friends and we do the same. We just meet each other for work!

Being one of the junior reporters at *The News* I was asked to cover all the Page 3 parties. I didn't like the job because one worked hard, trying to get as much *gossip* as possible, and wouldn't even get a byline for it. Ergo, no one really knew what you were doing. And one had to be out late in the night, almost every weekend, to cover some party or the other. Given a choice, I would be partying with my friends and family rather than hanging around at some Bollywood birthday.

It was the start of the new millennium but the film industry functioned in a tradional way. Film producers would throw parties and call the press, expecting the event to be covered in the newspapers. Everyone thought that I was enjoying this. But I now wonder who was really enjoying and with whom? Actors didn't stay back at the parties where we were invited. They cut the red ribbon or released the audio cassette of the film music, smiled for the cameras and vanished. And we were left with fellow journalists. Now, if we had to party with our journalist friends we could have done that at the Press Club or some other place. How could we *enjoy* at a producer's do where the actors walked in two to three hours late to promote their own film.

In spite of all this, I became a regular at these parties and made friends with reporters of other newspapers who covered the same events. Every night, after covering an event at a five star, I had to take a bus and travel all the way to Chembur and return to the office around noon, the next day, to file the story and then rush off to a new hotel to cover a new party.

My family and friends thought I was having a lot of fun in life; late nights attending *filmi* parties and hobnobbing with celebrities. I just smiled because it was hard to explain that this was not really worth it.

The next day the producer's office would call to find out when the event would get featured in the newspaper, and hound us till we gave them some space on our Bollywood page.

Fortunately, this is not the case with new age filmmakers, but the old timers were publicity hungry.

Earlier, in the late '90s, producers used to distribute gifts at events, which even included articles like dinner sets and pressure cookers, apart from the merchandise of the film, like T-shirts, caps and pens with the name of the film and banner on it. A section of the media would trip over each other to grab this.

One of the top producers of Bollywood, Vasant Bhagnani, who has worked with some top stars kept his annual party just before Diwali. It was a good time to be in the news as he would announce a film on the same day in the presense of the media. Celebrity guests would include the cast of his forthcoming film and some of those who had worked with him in the past. A regular cake cutting ceremony and a short press conference was followed by dinner and drinks at a five star hotel. He was known to give good gifts to the media. The first year I attended his do, he was giving away pressure cookers. I was too embarrassed to go the counter, register and carry back home a big box with a pressure cooker! But there were many tripping over each other to get it. A few of us were sitting at a table nearby, having dinner and watching all the fun.

Suddenly, Bhanu Mehta, a well-known film journalist, clad in a saree, got up and decided to take her gift. But she had to fight her way through the swarm of journalists and photographers. While she was walking by the swimming pool and smiling at someone, a couple of photographers, squabbling over one box, were walking towards her. Neither of them noticed her. The next thing we saw was Bhanu Mehta in the swimming pool. Not just that…the box with the heavy pressure cooker had landed on her. Everything came to a standstill. Some of the photographers and waiters pulled her out. Embarassed and soaked to the toe, she was almost in tears and must have felt extremely embarrassed. People around were trying to control their laughter.

Producer Vasant Bhagnani called for one of his cars and told the driver to drop her home.

For a few days, Bhanu Mehta was the talk of the media industry; every journalist, in their respective office, was discussing it. Even at *The News,* Rajeev and other journalists came up to me to ask what had actually happened. There were several others, like Bhavesh, the loudmouth photographer, who joked about the incident for days at end.

That was not the end. A few days later, at another party, when Bhanu Mehta walked in, someone from a group of photographers shouted, 'Bhanu*ji sambhalo!* Swimming pool! (Bhanu*ji*, be careful! There is a swimming pool here!)'

Seething, she turned towards the group and responded, '*Har**i! Apni maa ko jaake bol!* (Bas***ds! Go and tell your mom that!)' She then walked away.

Most of the times, I was the only one representing my newspaper during these parties. I remember going to Enigma, a discotheque inside hotel JW Marriott, for several parties and music release functions. The areas where the celebrities would sit and drink, was usually cordoned off and well-secured by the bouncers. Drinks were on the house but I certainly didn't enjoy drinking alone. So I would sometimes order a pint beer and hold it till I left the place. The only time we media would get a glimpse of the stars was when they headed to the washrooms. The dark interiors of the discotheque otherwise made it impossible to even see the person next to us. At times, I got thoroughly bored, but had to stay on to justify a tiny write-up the next day.

That was the time, at the turn of the century, when cell phones were just coming into use. People who owned the gadget would often flaunt it by tapping away on the keys or trying to speak loudly into their cell phone in the din around them.

Next morning, at tea, my mom would invariably ask me where I was the previous night. Sipping my tea and glancing through the newspaper I would say that I was at a party which had stars like Shah Rukh Khan, Karan Johar, Preity Zinta, among others. My mom, who is faster than any media house in the world, would do the honours of spreading the news to my extended family! She obviously felt very proud of her son's *achievement*.

One day I reached office and my cell phone beeped. '*Wow! These days you are partying with Shah Rukh Khan! Great going Raghu. I am very happy for you*,' wrote my cousin.

I wondered how I could explain to my family that it was anything but fun. But I guess they would not be able to picture my situation of sitting alone at a bar in a strange Bollywood party.

One night I had to stay back late in the office to make the pages for a special issue. My phone rang at 2 a.m. It was my mom.

'*Beta, do baj gaye hain. Kidhar ho? Koi actor ke saath ho kya*?' she asked.

'No mom,' I said exasperatedly, and added, 'I am sitting and making pages in office because day after tomorrow is a holiday and we have to get the pages done before that.'

But after a point I stopped making an effort to explain things to them. I told myself that if the thought of me partying with film stars would make my family, especially my mom, happy then I should probably just let it be.

After speaking to fellow reporters I came to the conclusion that nobody enjoyed these parties. Usually, we were first asked to wait and sometimes just informed that the star just wouldn't talk to anyone as he/she had a flight to catch. If the event was being handled by a good PR company then they managed to convince the star to give a collective interview to all the reporters present.

I had heard that there was once a time when a handful of top journalists were invited to an actor's private party but now even that didn't happen. I don't blame the stars for not inviting any journalists for their parties. Even if they did, the ones who had been left out would hound them with repeated phone calls and text messages. These reporters were under constant pressure from their bosses. Every boss wanted their reporter to be invited to the most happening party.

Deven Sampath was a journalist who, like me, reported on the entertainment beat. I had noticed the way he would gatecrash most of these parties. He would dress up for the occasion and wait outside. As soon as a luxury car stopped at the entrance he would walk up to the celebrity and start talking. He created an impression that he had just walked out and was casually walking back in, while talking to the celebrity. If you are all dressed up and walk into a party with a celebrity, you will obviously not be stopped by the security. In this way, he would get all the inside gossip from these parties. His party coverage was becoming popular and catching the eye of all editors.

Rajeev called me once, 'Raghu, everyone is wondering how Deven gets the entire scoop from these parties. If he is invited for all the big parties then how are we being left out? We are missing out on a lot of interesting information for our copies.'

'Rajeev, he is an unabashed gatecrasher.'

'What? Are you serious? How can he just land up uninvited?'

I explained Deven's modus operandi.

'That is really shocking,' Rajeev looked horrified. 'We should never resort to this.'

Rajeev was thoughtful for a while and then he said.

'But do one thing. When you call the stars who attended the party and are willing to talk, then also let them in on this little bit of information. Let's beat Deven at his own game.'

The usual practice I followed was that after every party I called a few actors; the not so popular ones but who were media savvy. They were happy to share information about the party as long as we also put their names or photos. The next time, while talking to them about the party, I spread the word that this particular journalist gatecrashes every party.

The word spread and the Khans, who threw the biggest parties in the city, informed their security that Deven Sampath should not be allowed to enter. After a couple of embarrassing moments in front of his colleagues in the media, when he was stopped at the entrance to a party and asked to show an invite, Deven stopped his cheap trick.

We didn't see him gatecrashing after that and suddenly the party pages lost all the spice; only photos and no gossip.

For me, the good thing that came out of this was that at the insistence of my boss I worked twice as hard for my stories and that included striving to get the extra gossip that people loved to read.

In the initial days of my career, I used to attend *filmi* parties, which were then primarily held at the two popular hotels, Centaur and Sun N Sand. Once the party was over I would hop across to the bus stop to catch BEST bus no. 352 that took me straight to Chembur, right outside my house near RK Studio.

At times, I would feel embarrassed standing at the bus stop, wondering what Shah Rukh Khan or any other celebrity would think if they passed by in their car and saw me standing at the bus stop; considering I had been to the same party, as them, a short while ago. So I used to stand at a little distance to avoid embarrassment.

Sitting in a BEST bus, after spending hours at a five star hotel and seeing film stars, was when the reality would hit me—the five-star part was just my job. I was the guy who travelled to Chembur, in a BEST bus, on a ticket of Rs 5. In a span of few hours I was tossed from one extreme to another; a five star one with glitz and glamour and the most expensive alcohol flowing like water, to the world where people were returning home after a hard day's work, dozing off and then waking up with a sudden jerk as the bus put on the brakes. There were times when sheer fatigue made me sleep; so I missed my stop in Chembur and landed at the depot in Deonar, only to be woken up by the conductor. I had to then get off, cross the road and take a bus, back two stops, to get home.

When people saw the newspapers or saw clippings of the parties, they thought these were the best parties in town. What could be more brilliant than parties where popular faces of the film industry hung around? But the reality was something else—these parties were fake, as were the smiles and air kisses.

I often wondered why I continued to work here, despite the fact that I had begun to hate Bollywood with each passing day. Ironical though it was, it was because that was the only industry I knew from the time I had started working.

5

Meeting an Underworld Don

The underworld had always fascinated me. From watching movies based on underworld dons to reading books on the famous Mumbai gang wars, I had always fed my interest. Vinod Khanna's *Dayavan*, Amitabh Bachchan's *Agneepath*, Ajay Devgn's *Company* and Sanjay Dutt's *Vaastav* were my favourite films and I watched them everytime they were telecast on TV. I took great interest in news on the underworld; whether it was of an underworld goon being shot in an encounter or any such nefarious elements who were on the run. I kept a tab on all the developments of the underworld that made headlines, the arrest and deportation of don Abu Salem was fascinating, I didn't expect him to be so decent looking.

When I joined *The News*, Dey used to handle the crime beat; he was a big name in crime journalism. He would often talk of all his experiences about meeting encounter specialists and even some local dons in Mumbai. Like I was fascinated with the underworld, Dey's interest was Bollywood.

Dey and I had a deal where he had said, 'Some day you take me to meet Aamir Khan and I will make you meet an underworld don!'

I prayed that the opportunity arrived soon when I would get to meet an underworld don in flesh and blood. It is thanks to Dey, that I was fully updated with the news from the crime world.

One day I asked him, 'Dey, why don't you try and interview Dawood Ibrahim?'

'Do you think it is that easy?'

I egged him on saying that he would surely be able to manage one if he tried hard enough.

He laughed, '*Itna easy hota to har crime* reporter Dawood *ka* interview *karta na! Zindagi mein ek baar dekhne bhi mil gaya to bhi badi baat hogi. Soch woh* Dubai *mein hai, yaa* Pakistan *mein, yaa kidhar aur, woh bhi humko pata nahi hai.*' (Had it been this easy, then all crime reporters would be doing stories on Dawood. It will be an achievement if I get to even see him. We don't even know if he is in Dubai or Pakistan.)'

Dey explained further, 'Raghu, he is Dawood Ibrahim; not a small-time thief. I cannot dial his number and expect him to answer my questions. He is an international figure. Why should he care for some local publicity? Think about it—in these many years he has not done a single interview. And what do you think he would say, even if he agrees to an interview?

'You are watching too many Hindi films. Be happy with the *filmi* dons we get to see on a regular basis,' he joked.

'Does that mean that you will not introduce me to a real-life don?'

'I said I will introduce you to a don; not to Dawood Ibrahim.'

'Okay, okay, a local don then. But I should be given five to seven minutes to chat with him,' I said, realising that my desire to see Dawood in the flesh had just gone up in smoke.

'Five to seven minutes! Once you meet a don you will be shitting bricks. You will be meeting him in his territory, surrounded by his bodyguards. There will be thorough checking. The bravest ones get scared once they are in front of a don.'

A week after this discussion, Dey called me at 10 p.m. I was home, watching TV and finishing dinner with family.

'*Oye! Kidhar hai tu?* (Hey! Where are you?)'

I responded that I was at home.

'*Chal raat ko ek baje Dongri mein mil.* (Meet me at Dongri at 1 a.m.)'

'What? At 1 a.m… In Dongri!' I was taken by surprise.

'Do you want to meet a don or no?' Dey asked.

I could feel my pulse race. Me…actually meet a don? But how…where?

There were several questions racing through my mind, but I was able to let out only a few.

'Yes, yes…of course! But which don? And where is Dongri?'

'You live in Chembur right. Meet me at 12:30 a.m. outside Sion Hospital. I will pick you up from there.'

The initial excitement was slowly giving way to a fear of the unknown.

'But who are we meeting? That too this late in the night. Is it safe?'

Dey laughed out aloud and said, 'You want to meet a don and you want it to be safe!'

I was taken aback at Dey's response.

He said finally, '*Sab* safe *hai*. Come over and don't wear flashy clothes—just simple jeans and T-shirt. And don't tell anyone where you are going.'

Mom and Reena had both heard me saying *don* a couple of times over the phone. They were ready with their questions as soon as I disconnected the call.

Reena asked eagerly, 'Hey dude! What is it? Who was it? Why were you talking about some don?'

I looked at mom and could sense the same eagerness in her expression.

'*Arre*... Dey is meeting some don. I had told him that I too wanted to meet one...'

'No need,' mom said in a firm voice. I knew that when she was angry like this, there was no way of getting through to her.

Reena was more verbose, 'Are you mad dude! Don't even think about it. What if there is trouble? What if...'

'Okay, okay relax. I won't go.'

I was in a fix. I had to leave in some time and both women at home had given their verdict. I knew that I would have to resort to lying to step out of the house at this hour. So, after feighning a phone call, I told them that Rajeev was coming to Chembur for some work and I had to step out to have coffee with him. Rajeev's name worked as a trump card in my house; they trusted him blindly. I didn't bother telling Rajeev because I knew they would not be checking with him.

As I left the house mom only said, '*Beta*, get Rajeev home someday. Tell him to come over for tea.'

'Yes mom, I'll tell him,' and trying to sound convincing, added, 'When he has some time I will get him along.'

It was 11 p.m. and I had remembered to step out in casual, inconspicuous clothes. It was late in the night and the frequency of the buses had also fallen considerably. After about half an hour I got a BEST Bus No. 90, which dropped me right outside Sion Hospital. I looked at my watch, which said midnight. Now I had to wait for Dey.

At 12:30 a.m. a bike skidded to a halt just ahead of me. It had missed me by inches. It was only when the man took off his helmet that I recognised him as Dey.

'*Chal baith. Aaj teri icha puri karta hoon.* (Hop on! Let me fulfil your wish today.)'

I hopped on and covered my face with a handkerchief as instructed.

'Where are we going? Who are we meeting? Tell me something,' I was really excited.

'*Dongri ke don Abu Bhai se.* (We are going to meet the Don of Dongri, Abu Bhai.)' Dey said with elan.

'Wow!'

'Just make sure you don't tell anyone about this. Don't get me into trouble,' Dey warned.

We zoomed through the new flyovers at Dadar and Parel and reached Dongri in 20 minutes flat.

'Switch off your mobile. You are not allowed to use it here,' came Dey's next instruction.

'If my phone is switched off then my mom will get worried,' I told him frantically. The truth was that at this point I did not want to close that one point of contact with the rest of the world. What if there was trouble? What if I needed to make a call urgently?'

'She will be more worried if the don shoots you,' Dey snapped.

'I will keep it on silent. No one will find out.'

As I put my phone on silent, Dey called someone from his mobile, 'Yes I have reached. Where are you?'

We waited for the person who would be taking us to meet Abu Bhai.

'I have some work with him. I think he has to give me some news. You sit quietly after I have introduced you and don't worry,' Dey assured me.

A short while later, a young boy, not more than 25-years-old and in white *kurta pyjama*, arrived. Dey hugged him.

He looked at me and asked with a smile, 'Is he the film reporter?'

For the next 10 minutes or so we walked through the narrow lanes and bylanes of Dongri. I could barely see anything around me; just followed the sound of footsteps in front of me. I now understood why this particular hour had been chosen for the meeting—we would never be able to find our way back here, even in broad daylight.

We finally reached a building which had very high walls. The guy knocked on the door, I noticed, thrice. Must be a signal, I told myself, remembering similar scenarios in some of the Bollywood films I had seen. Someone looked out of the window, above the entrance and the door was opened for us. They were obviously expecting us, I guessed.

An armed guard checked us thoroughly, instructing us to leave our mobiles in the plastic box he handed to us. We could pick it up on our way out.

I silently followed the instructions—I wasn't going to argue here as I had earlier with Dey.

We walked up to the first floor and went through another round of security; this time with a metal detector. Once they were sure that we were clean, we were taken forward through many doors and corridors to finally stop in a huge open sitting area decorated with plush furniture. We sat on the couch to wait for Abu Bhai.

I looked on with some alarm as several men came to meet Dey.

After several pensive minutes, for me in particular, a well-built person walked in, in a *pathani* suit with a lot of gold around his neck and wrists and asked with a smile, 'What will you have? Tea or whiskey?'

Dey responded, 'Tea would be okay.'

'And this kid is the film reporter, right?' The man looked at me and asked.

I stood staring at the man who I guessed was Abu Bhai, the Don of Dongri. His persona sure made me feel that he ruled over the people I now saw around me, and the locality at large.

Dey's next words however came as a surprise.

'Yes like I told you. He works with me so I brought him along. I have informed big brother. He said it is okay.'

The man looked at me with a smile, which I thought was of assurance, and said, 'No problem. He meets reel heroes everyday. Today he will get to meet a real hero.'

'Hmm...' was all I could manage as fear gripped me. How much more formidable would the real Don of Dongri be?

We were having tea and biscuits, when a good-looking man in jeans and T-shirt walked in. I noticed the reverence on the faces of the men who stood in the room and guessed that I was finally meeting the man I had set out to meet. He looked absolutely fit and fresh. He could have been an actor.

He hugged Dey and said, 'Dey, you have become so thin. Does your wife not feed you properly?' and then turning to me said, 'Hey! How are things in your Bollywood? Everyone there is my friend. Should I tell you the names of my friends in Bollywood?'

But the banter made way for serious business. Abu Bhai wanted to meet Dey for a specific reason.

'Dey, you are my friend, so I am telling you this. Ramesh Dhoble is your friend, right?'

'You mean that crime reporter from the Marathi newspaper?' Dey asked.

'Yes. Tell that son of a bitch that I know what he is upto,' Abu Bhai thundered, making me want to shrink further into the couch.

Dey however looked confused, 'I don't understand. What is he upto?'

'He has taken money from our rival gang and is writing rubbish about me on a daily basis.'

Just then one of the security guys handed a file to him.

'See this; five stories last month and already two stories this month and it's only the beginning of the month.'

Dey took the file, which I now noticed had newspaper cuttings and started flipping through the articles.

'I will kill him I am telling you,' Abu Bhai's eyes flashed anger, completely transforming his good looks that I had admired earlier. He now cut a menacing figure and I was glad that Ramesh Dhoble was not my friend.

'No, no! I will talk to him and explain things to him,' Dey offered.

I just sat listening to the conversation. I couldn't believe that this kind of open threat could be issued right in the heart of a metropolitan city, which is known to have one of the most efficient army of law enforcers.

Then just as suddenly the don decided to change his tactic. 'Tell him if he wants money I will give it to him. But this has to stop immediately.'

'Yes, I will speak to him tomorrow,' Dey assured.

'If he does one more story against me, I will not stop to think that he is a journalist; I will treat him the same way as I treat my enemies. I have been trying to keep my image clean because I am trying to get a ticket for the elections.

This idiot is coming in my way; he is determined to ruin my image.'

Dey once again promised to have a word with his friend, although I wondered if he was now regretting this friendship.

'So tell me, how is your editor?' the don said suddenly, changing the topic.

'He is fine,' Dey answered.

'*Arrey*, who are you trying to fool? He is definitely not fine. I heard your newspaper doesn't have any money. They are looking for investors and if they don't find one in a few months, then they would have to sell the newspaper.'

'Abu Bhai, these stories have been circulating for years now. Don't believe any of this. Our newspaper is doing well.'

'Okay, if you say so…'

Now that the matter at hand had been attended to, Abu Bhai turned his attention to me. 'So! How are the heroines doing? Do you meet them?'

'I meet them sometimes.'

'Yesterday a top actress called me. Some estate agent was troubling her for money. I called him once and now the actress is sleeping tight.'

There was silence in the room, so he continued, 'Madam had bought a house for four crores but didn't pay the agent his commission. So, he went after her and she came running to me.'

I had only heard of such things happening in the movies. I mustered up the courage and asked, 'Which heroine are you talking about?'

There was an awkward silence in the room. Dey kicked me under the table. Oh God! Maybe I shouldn't have asked him the question. I felt like kicking myself now.

'Hey film reporter? Do you think I will really tell you who she is? So that you go and publish it.'

And then suddenly, he stood up, which caused the rest of us to also jump to our feet.

He hugged Dey and then hugged me, saying, 'I like you. You are brave. Come again with Dey.'

'Yes, will surely come…Sir,' I stuttered, balking at the idea of going through this again.

'This is not an office where you call people sir. Call me *bhai*,' he said with elan.

'Yes, *bhai*, I will come,' I said, trying to sound enthusiastic about the idea.

'*Chalo khuda hafiz…*'

We were escorted out of the building. As we were walking down through the dark lanes again, Dey whispered to me, 'Are you mad? Never ask a don a question like that. Thank God Abu Bhai was in a good mood.'

As we picked up our phones I noticed three missed calls from my mother. It was 1:30 a.m. now.

I called back, 'Yes mom, I am on my way home. You go to sleep, I have the key.'

Phew! We sat on the bike and headed out towards the highway.

'Okay hero! Are you happy now? Now don't go and tell the whole world about this,' Dey told me as I stepped off his bike.

'Of course not. It was great fun, Dey. You know him so well. He called us inside, gave us tea and spoke so politely.'

'When they need you for some work, they will do everything. They are bas***ds, nothing else. Now, you have to introduce me to Aamir Khan,' he said thumping me on my back.

'Definitely!'

He was heading towards Ghatkopar so I asked him to drop me off somewhere, where I would get an auto to Chembur.

Later, as the auto drove through the quiet lanes of the suburban neighbourhood, my mind flew back to the last hour. I still couldn't believe that I had met Abu Bhai. People only read about him in the newspapers and I had tea with him!

Dey and I did not discuss this episode again, even though we met at work almost everyday.

A week later, when all the reporters were having lunch in the office canteen, Dey got a call. Since he was the crime reporter he was obviously the first in our office to know about a crime in the city. He sauntered off to a quiet corner of the room to talk.

'*Kya baat kar raha hai*?' he said aloud, causing many of us to turn towards him.

It was definitely some big news. We waited for him to tell us what had happened.

'Top film actress Neha Kumar was shot dead in Lokhandwala, Andheri, by an estate agent. Apparently she owed him some money. Four rounds were fired at her and she died instantly. The estate agent is absconding,' he told us.

I was shocked. I had connected the dots in my mind. Dey gave me a look which clearly implied that I should not open my mouth. He soon left the office; this was breaking news. Such an incident had never happened before. Rajeev asked me to get the reaction of actors and actresses. So I too was out of the office minutes after Dey; he to get the facts and me for all the gossip surrounding it.

What a bizarre place this industry is, I tell myself, she bought a house worth crores but wanted to save a few lakhs, and that cost her... *Her life*!

6

My First Big Story

I had done many stories on Bollywood but the one that got me fame was the one on yesteryears filmstar Parveen Babi.

Once a top star in Bollywood, it was now common knowledge that she had become mentally unsound. Members of the film fraternity had distanced themselves from her. In 2002, some gossip magazines wrote about her mental condition and it was picked up by the other glossies. It is ironic that when any star hits a low it makes for good copy.

Since magazines had done stories on her without speaking to the actress herself, I was told to try and get an interview with her. Rajeev urged me to give it my best shot.

He said, 'Call her landline and take it from there.'

I knew that I had to crack this one… It was my first big opportunity.

As I was about to dial the landline, I wondered what I was going to say if someone picked up the phone.

No one answered the phone. Later, of course, I found out that she rarely did.

After some enquiry with senior film journalists I managed to find the address of her building in Juhu. She owned the penthouse apartment of the building, Rovela Apartments, and it faced the Arabian Sea.

Since she didn't answer the phone, the only option was to land up at her doorstep. When I reached the building, the watchman asked, as is the policy with almost all buildings in Mumbai, 'Who are you visiting?'

'Parveen Babi,' I responded, trying to sound confident.

The man laughed out aloud and asked, 'Has she called you?'

'No. I mean… Yes, she has called me.'

'How? She called you over the phone?' He asked smiling and chewing his *paan*. Finally, sensing my irritation, he directed me to the elevator.

I reached the top floor and rang the doorbell of the only flat there.

No response.

I stood there in the eerie silence of the corridor. Milk packets and newspapers were lying outside the door and I became aware of a weird smell. I rang the doorbell a couple of times more, but the door remained closed. I could hear the sound of scuffling feet on the other side of the door. Was she looking at me through the magic eye? I rang the bell again and finally decided to leave.

The watchman asked me cheekily, 'What happened? Did you meet Parveen Babi?'

'No one opened the door.'

'She doesn't open the door to anyone,' he informed me, before saying, 'Are you a filmstar that she will invite you into her flat?'

I ignored the watchman's jibe and decided to gather some information.

'Does she step out of her flat? Have you seen her?'

'I have been here for two years now. I have never seen her. I only know that she lives on the top floor.'

'So you haven't seen her in two years?' I repeated just to be sure that I have got my facts right.

'I would be able to see her only if she comes out, right?' The watchman said, sounding irritated.

'What about her food and groceries?' I asked.

'A young girl comes in the evening. She runs all the errands for Parveen Babi.'

I wondered whether I should return in the evening to meet the girl. Maybe I should ask the watchman to request the girl to wait here for me. I took my press card out of my bag to tell him who I was and he immediately said, 'Why don't you go and try again, Sir. She might just open the door.'

The press card had worked; his tone had mellowed. I went up to the apartment again and rang the doorbell a couple of times.

Suddenly a shrill voice spoke out from behind the door, 'Who are you? Who do you want to meet?'

Parveen Babi!

By now I was petrified and wanted to run down the stairs, perhaps because of the stories I had heard about her being of an unsound mind. But the reporter in me spoke out, 'Ma'am, this is Raghu from *The News*. I want to interview you.'

'Go away! I am not doing any interviews. Who has sent you? You can't just come to my door Mr Raghu. Call me tomorrow at 10 a.m. My number is 2642821.'

I kept staring at the magic eye because I knew that she was looking at me.

'You can leave now,' she shouted.

'Yes...yes ma'am... Thank...thank you!'

I didn't bother waiting for the elevator and I just ran down seven floors and kept looking back to see if I was being followed.

The watchman saw me rushing out, and called out, 'What happened? Did you get to see her?'

I brushed past him as I responded, not daring to stop, 'Yes, yes! I heard her voice. That's enough for me.'

I acknowledged that this was an unnatural fear; fear of this persona that the media had created of her—it was ironical that being a journalist I too was prone to it.

The next morning I called Parveen Babi at 10 a.m. on the dot.

She answered after one bell with a 'Hello!'

'Ma'am, this is Raghu… I had come to see you yesterday.'

'What do you want? I don't do interviews Mr Raghu, don't you know that?'

'Ma'am… Please… If you could make an exception and do one good interview…'

She interrupted me, 'What do you know about me Mr… er… Raghu.'

I was taken aback by the question. Should I dare to mouth all that was being written about her in the film glossies? That is assuming she hadn't been following the stories. What if she had?

'Quite a bit ma'am, actually… quite a lot,' I said finally.

'Read up as much as you can about me and come tomorrow at 3 p.m. I will give you an interview. Hope you will come alone?'

'Ma'am, I will come with my photographer.'

'Okay Raghu, I am trusting you because you sound genuine. See you tomorrow at 3 p.m. You and your photographer and no one else, okay…'

'Yes, ma'am.'

I hung up and rushed to Rajeev to give him the good news.

Rajeev is impressed, 'Wow! An exclusive interview with the recluse Parveen Babi. That's awesome! Great job.'

Without hesitation I can say that this story made me a journalist. The emotional ups and downs I went through during the course of the interview are difficult to describe.

From what I remember of my growing up years, Parveen Babi was so beautiful, so different from what she was now. Sitting across the table with the yesteryear's superstar, I realised she was so out of touch with reality; it shook me completely.

The dining table was full of stacks of paper, mostly hand-written affidavits. Old clothes and hand towels were strewn on the floor as far as our eyes could see. The sofa cover was torn; she obviously never let anyone in to change it.

She peppered her conversations with an oft-repeated line, 'Raghu, I have no friends.' She would mention this, again and again, as long as I was there. My eyes grew moist and I felt my insides wrench every time she said that.

Once a superstar who would do films only opposite A-list stars and had fans tripping over each other for one glance or one smile, she was now somebody who had no friends. I asked her, 'Ma'am, what went wrong? Where did your friends go? Why don't you go out and meet them?'

She looked at me directly in the eye and said, 'If I move out they will kill me. There are shooters on the lookout for me. I have seen them follow me. I somehow ran home and saved myself a couple of times but some day they will get me.'

I asked her who would want to kill her and why? She had no answers. She just kept repeating herself.

With every passing minute, I became aware of the oppressive atmosphere in the house. It was a house facing the beautiful Arabian Sea, but the windows were shut because of the fear of death and this, together with the nervousness I could sense about her, made it stifling. The smell of fear was more overpowering than the smell in the house which was because the windows had not been opened in years.

Before the interview she took a photograph each of my cameraman Mohan Bhai and me and we both looked at each other wondering what she was going to do with them. We spent three hours in her house and my head hurt from seeing the papers, affidavits, documents which were meant to prove that she was in good mental health; how could she have written them otherwise. I nodded but I wasn't convinced. Nobody would be convinced if they saw her. She offered me tea but I was scared to drink it. When we were leaving she asked for our visiting cards. I didn't have one and Mohan Bhai lied with a straight face that he was not carrying his. Later, he told me he was scared to share his contact details with her.

When we finally left, I promised myself that I would stay in touch with her; perhaps a part of me wanted to take on the responsibility of helping her separate fact from delusion. Mohan Bhai and I did not say a word to each other as we took our respective mode of transport home.

When I went to work the next day, I didn't know how to structure the information—I had so much to write. My story was the front page lead of *The News* the next day. I got many compliments and calls. Everyone I bumped into, at work in particular, told me what a great read it was. But

I was uncomfortable. I wanted to know what Parveen Babi thought about my story.

Rajeev told me that I should call and check and I admitted to him that I was scared. Since there was no other way, I dialed her number. A maid answered the phone to say that she was busy and could not take the call.

I knew she was avoiding my call. Ridden with guilt I did not get good sleep that night. What if she felt betrayed by my story? She thought that the world out there was plotting to kill her…did she now think that I was one of them?

Next morning when I reached office the editor told me there was a 100 page notice, from Parveen Babi to the newspaper. It said, '*Your reporter Raghu Kumar had come with the intention of killing me. He is connected with the underworld…*' There were other things too that didn't make sense.

Everyone in office tried to explain that it was not my fault; she was not of sound mind and that she would have reacted to any story in the same way. But I could not get over the guilt; I had become too attached to this story.

As the work stress built up steadily, it began to take its toll on me. I realised that I needed a break. I asked my family if they would like to visit Lonavala over a weekend. They were happy with my idea and the three of us spent the weekend at a hotel facing the Bushi Dam.

After I returned, I told myself that a news story was just that…a story that needed to be told. I promised myself that there would be no more emotional attachments thereafter.

A few years after I did the story, Parveen Babi was found dead in the same apartment. I was assigned to do the story and visited the hospital where her body was kept. Medical reports suggested that she had died a few days before her body was discovered and it came to light because the neighbours complained of foul smell. A photographer had managed to get some closeup shots of the dead body that was kept inside the morgue. It was unclaimed for days because she didn't have any immediate family and she was not in touch with any of her relatives. He showed me the pictures. I couldn't believe what I saw. It was a terrible and tragic end of a glamorous heartthrob. Once a beauty to die for, she had fallen on the wayside. Very few people came to pay their condolences. How fickle the film industry was, I wondered.

I once again realised how much I hated Bollywood.

That night I went out with a group of friends from the media and told them about my experience with Parveen Babi. Her death confirmed yet again that once an actor was out of business no one cared whether they lived or died.

'Man! This industry is the worst place to be in, I must say,' a friend echoed my sentiments as we called it a day.

7

The Television Boom

Post 2002, quite a few print reporters got offers from TV channels. It was the same job, the only difference being that you had to speak your words in front of the camera, instead of writing them out in a newspaper. It was the dream of every journalist to work for News 24x7, the only news channel that was ruling the television scene then. The advantages that came with a News 24x7 press card were endless. I too sent my resume to the channel when I heard they were hiring people.

On February 12, 2003, a group of journalists were taken from Mumbai to Wai to cover the shoot of the Ajay Devgan film *Gangajal*. I was representing my newspaper. We reached in three hours and checked in at our hotel at 8:30 a.m.

Junkets in those days were great fun. We would travel together in a bus, catch up on gossip and exchange notes with other reporters and get information about other media houses. On this two-day trip we had to share rooms with our respective photographers. So I was sharing my room with Mohan Bhai.

When we had checked into our rooms, Mohan Bhai went for a bath and I decided to lie down and rest for a while. Just then my new cell phone rang. It was a Delhi number. I answered.

'Hi is this Mr Raghu Kumar?'

'Yes, speaking.'

'I am calling from News 24x7. The editors of the channel would like to see you today. Please be present at our Andheri office at 4 p.m. It will be a video interview, since the editors are in Delhi.'

I panicked immediately.

'But ma'am, I am in Wai. Are interviews happening only today?'

'Yes. So will you be able to make it or should I cancel yours?'

I had to think fast.

So after a five-second pause, I said, 'Yes, yes, I will be present.'

I disconnected my cell phone. Mohan Bhai was standing in front of me. 'What happened? Who was on the phone?' he asked.

I decided to come to the point directly, 'Mohan Bhai, I got an interview call from News 24x7, but the interview has been scheduled for 4 p.m. today and that too in Andheri, Mumbai.'

'So tell them that you are in Wai and won't be able to make it today. Ask them to have the interview tomorrow.'

'Mohan Bhai, this is my golden opportunity to join a TV news channel. If they hire someone else, I may not even get another chance. An interview has been scheduled with the main editors, Kranti, Sukanya and Alok Mittal; all the big guys in Delhi.'

'But, didn't you just say that the interview was in Andheri, Mumbai?' Mohan Bhai asked, looking confused.

I was getting irritated with his questions as I could not see a solution in hand.

'It's a video interview,' I said in exasperation. 'They would be in Delhi and I, in Mumbai. The interview would be done through a video link.'

'Wow! News 24x7 sure does things in style.'

He seemed lost in thought for a while. I knew he was genuinely concerned for me. Then he suddenly stated, 'You do one thing. You leave now. I will tell them you had fallen sick and had to leave urgently. I will click the photos and take all the information. You file the story and don't tell anyone about this. Don't take any tension about the coverage here.'

I knew this would be cheating on the job. But I also knew that this was an opportunity of a lifetime. I hugged Mohan Bhai as he wished me luck and left the hotel.

There was no transport available around the hotel so I had to walk for three kilometres to reach a bus stand. From there I took a bus to the main bus depot to get a bus to Mumbai.

I called my mom from my cell phone, asking her to iron my formal white shirt and my trousers. She bombarded me with questions which I promised to answer when I reached home. I was not in the frame of mind to talk now. I was excited and tensed!

I managed to reach the main depot, buy the ticket and board the bus heading for Mumbai, just as it was about to depart. I got a seat and thanked my stars that I had not missed this one or I would have had to wait for another hour for the next one. I was out of Wai at around 10:30 a.m.

On the way, I prayed that I would get this job. Thankfully, Chembur is one of the first localities as one entered Mumbai from Wai. I was home at 1:30 p.m. ringing the doorbell continuously till my mom opened the door.

My sister shouted, 'Stop ringing the doorbell like this. I am on the phone, you idiot!'

I had no time to react to her. I stormed into the house, 'I have to get ready and go to News 24x7 for an interview with the top editors.'

My sister hung up as she heard News 24x7.

I gave her a job as I got ready, 'Log on to the net and find out the address of the News 24x7 office in Andheri.'

My sister, who always had questions, now asked, 'But didn't they give you the address? Didn't you ask them for the address?'

I shouted back in exasperation, even though I risked letting in the shaving foam into my mouth, 'Are you helping me with this or not? I don't have time.'

She connected to the internet through our dial up connection, which always took time to connect.

When she finally handed me the chit of paper with the address, it also said, '*You will get the job*!'

I decided to take a cab to Andheri.

This was definitely the most action-packed birthday I was having. On one side I was mentally preparing myself for the interview and on the other side I was thinking about Mohan Bhai and the shoot in Wai and praying that that would go off smoothly. Mohan Bhai didn't have a cell phone so I had no way of finding out before he returned to Mumbai.

I reached the News 24x7 office at 3:45 p.m. I recognised some of the other reporters who had come for the interview. A lady was calling out our names and taking us to the studio, one at a time.

I gave her my name and she asked me to wait till my name was announced.

As I waited for my name to be called out, I couldn't believe that I didn't get time to prepare for such an important interview.

My name was finally called out and I was led into the studio.

'Have you done a video interview before this?' The lady asked me.

'Actually… No,' I stuttered, already nervous.

'Don't worry. Just follow the instructions of the man managing the camera and please switch off your cell phone.'

I switched off my Nokia and entered the studio. It was freezing inside.

The camera guy saw me, and introduced himself, 'Hi. I am Bhola. Please sit here and face the camera.'

He clipped a microphone on my shirt and shoved an ear piece into my ear.

'Mr Raghu, can you here me?' came a voice over the earphone.

'Yes sir, I can hear you. Who's this?'

'This is the Mumbai Production Control Room. We are just connecting you to our Delhi office.'

'Okay,' I responded, trying to sound confident.

'Hello Raghu, can you hear us?' Another voice spoke over the earphone.

'Yes, I can.'

'Okay. There are five of us here—Kranti, Alok Mittal Sir, Sukanya, our production head Priyanka and me, Anaita.'

'Hello… Hello everyone.'

Someone from the other end asked, 'So Raghu, what can you tell us about yourself?'

That is easy, I told myself, 'I am a film journalist. I write for *The News*. Before that I used to write on education and civic issues.'

'But why did you shift from covering civic issues to entertainment?' asked another voice, which I recognised as one of Kranti Mittal, who I had seen so many times on television.

'Sir, I was just out of college and that was the first job that came my way, so I decided to give it a shot.'

'So what would you want to cover if you get a job with us—civic issues or entertainment?' asked Kranti.

'Sir, I can report on anything, but over the years I have made good contacts in Bollywood. So I guess it would make more sense to use my contacts for the channel and report on Bollywood.'

So can you get Shah Rukh Khan for us if we need him at 9 p.m. tonight?' It was Kranti again.

'I can try Sir,' I responded.

'Hi Raghu, this is Alok Mittal,' said another voice. 'Do you speak Hindi? Basically, I would like to know if you could be a bilingual reporter.'

'Yes sir, I can speak in Hindi.'

'Sukanya here, Raghu. Why would you want to switch from print to TV, Raghu? Hindi *mein jawab deejiye* please. (Answer in Hindi please.)'

I did so promptly, 'Ma'am, *mujhe lagta hai ki mai ek acha* TV reporter *ban sakta hoon*. (Ma'am, I think I will make a good TV reporter.)'

I didn't know what else to say.

Sukanya was going through my resume I guessed, as she was speaking to me, because she then asked me, 'Is it your birthday today?'

'Yes Ma'am,' I finally had a smile on my face.

'Oh! So sweet of you to have come for the interview on your birthday,' Sukanya said and I could sense the smile in her voice.

'Ma'am, I know how I made it to the interview. In the morning I was in Wai and now I am here in front of you.'

Everyone wished me a Happy Birthday and the interview came to an end.

As I stepped out a girl with short hair came out of the production control room and said, 'I think your birthday did it for you. Good luck anyway and Happy Birthday.'

I smiled and said thanks.

Back home, the guilt of lying to Rajeev Mehra, leaving the assignment in charge of Mohan Bhai, really troubled me. Rajeev was now a friend and I had let him down. But I was really excited and wanted to tell him about my interview. I knew he would be happy if I did well in my career. But I had left an assignment in the middle, so didn't have the guts to call him. I knew it was wrong.

I told my sister and mom about the video interview experience. They were eagerly waiting to hear about it.

'What will you tell Rajeev Mehra?' My sister quizzed me.

My mom added, 'I think you should tell him. He is a nice person. He will understand.'

'It's my birthday and I am tired now. Let's go out for dinner and not talk about all this.'

'*Arre*, but I have made your favourite mushroom *sabzi*...' mom protested.

'I would be home tomorrow. I will eat my favourite *sabzi* then.'

We went to Geeta Bhavan, a popular South Indian eatery in Chembur.

My sister started, 'We know all the reporters who are seen on News 24x7 channel. If you get a job there you would also be as popular as them. People will recognise you on the roads.'

'Yes, but let me get the job first. I wouldn't like to get my hopes high and then be upset later if it doesn't work out.'

I stayed up most of the night wondering about the Wai shoot. I didn't want to think about the result of the interview. I thought about Mohan Bhai and how he must have covered up for my absence and hoped that he had been able to accumulate all the necessary material.

The next day, early morning, the door bell rang. It was Mohan Bhai.

I wondered if I had just conjured him up, since I had been really thinking about him. So I stood looking at him for a few seconds before I realised what I was doing…

'Hey Mohan Bhai, how did you get my address? Come in.'

'You look like you have seen a ghost. I am no less than a reporter, boss. Found out from the office.'

I introduced him to my mom, when she served us *poha* and *chai*.

'Was everything okay in Wai, Mohan Bhai?'

'Yes, of course. Forget that! You tell me, how was your interview at News 24x7?' he asked eagerly.

'No. First you tell me what happened in Wai,' I insisted.

'*Arre*, nothing much. Everyone was busy doing their own thing. I told the PRO that you had fallen sick and had to leave. They felt really sorry for you. Ajay Devgan also found out and reprimanded the PRO for not giving you a car, to return to Mumbai, when you were unwell. The man responded saying that he did not know about it. Then everyone got back to work. Nothing else. I have written down the details of the scene being shot and also got you the quotes, written on paper.'

I thanked him profusely, 'Mohan Bhai, I am really grateful for this. If I get a job in News 24x7, it will be because of you.'

'You have to give me a treat then,' he said and got up to leave.

As I walked him out, I told him about the interview experience.

'Ask them for a fat package,' he suggested, before adding, 'I have heard that News 24x7 is spending a lot these days.'

'They didn't discuss any money,' I told him, wondering whether I should take this as an indication that they were not interested in hiring me.

'Maybe that will come up in the interview with the HR. It's a big company after all. It will work out for you. You will get the job.'

I really hoped that his confidence in me would be proved right and hugged him before he left.

Next morning, I reached office around noon. The first person I bumped into was Rajeev.

'Hey Raghu, how was your shoot?' he asked me enthusiastically.

'Nice! Very nice! I will just visit the washroom and then talk to you,' I responded, completely at a loss for words. I was never good at lying. So I decided to tell Rajeev the truth. So squaring my shoulder for the consequences of my confession, I approached him in his cubicle and asked him if we could step out for 10 minutes.

'Not now Raghu! I have to finish this page and then go for a Shah Rukh Khan interview.'

'No problem. Tomorrow then.'

'No. Let's chat when I am back in the office in the evening.'

Rajeev left the office soon after and I spent the whole day in trepidation. Would I get thrown out of my job? Would I lose a good friend?

It was late evening when I saw Rajeev enter the office. By this time I had decided that I would be open about everything, including my interview. Consequences be damned!

I reminded him that I wanted to talk to him and suggested that we go to the Udipi restaurant down the road because in the canteen someone or the other would surely join us at our table.

As we stepped out Rajeev asked me, 'So, are you planning to quit?'

'Let's sit and talk,' I told him.

We ordered *dosa* and he asked, 'Tell me. What do you want to talk about?'

I hesitated for a moment but then gathered the courage and told him how I had returned from the Wai assignment for another job interview. He smiled through it and said, 'You should avoid doing this but I understand you had no choice this time.'

He had a strange smile on his face as he said, 'It's funny that you are telling me this. I also would like to tell you something, but keep it to yourself. I have an offer from Planet TV and I am considering taking it up.'

News 24x7 and Planet TV were rivals.

I found myself making Rajeev feel guilty, in jest, of course, 'When were you going to tell me this?'

He smiled, 'You would have been one of the first people to know. In fact, I thought once I was set I would offer you a job.'

'If all goes well we will work in rival companies,' I pointed out, suddenly realising what the future might hold for us.

He responded, 'Doesn't matter. We all have to think of our future and our personal growth. Tell me if you get a job confirmation from News 24x7. It's a very big channel. I wanted to later offer you a job at Planet TV but why would you quit News 24x7 and join Planet TV? Anyway, let's see how it goes. You have to get through and I also have to work out my deal. Keep all this to yourself till then.'

An offer letter was waiting for me from News 24x7 when I logged on to my email that evening.

The salary they had offered me was double of what I was getting and the designation was that of a reporter. I told my mom and my sister and none of us could believe that it had actually happened. I was going to be a News 24x7 reporter!

I immediately called Rajeev.

'Hey, guess what? I got the offer letter. I have to join in a month's time. The package is double.'

By this time I was almost jumping on the bed with joy.

'Wow! Congrats Raghu. That was quick. Very good.'

'I just can't believe it.'

'So my loss is News 24x7's gain.'

'I can't thank you enough Rajeev. You gave me my first break, hence I have this offer today.'

Rajeev was quick to point out, 'No Raghu, you are a hardworking boy and always remember, good things happen to good people. Now go and celebrate, I will see you in the office tomorrow.'

There was an impromptu party at my place; cousins were called and cake was ordered. It was a long night of celebrations.

'Raghu, what did News 24x7 see in you?' My sister joked. But I knew that she was the happiest right now.

'*Arre* now you watch. I will be a star reporter one day and that day is not too far away.'

Rajeev greeted me with a hug when I saw him in the office the next day. I knew that he was genuinely happy for me. He took me to the editor.

'Mr Ranjan, our reporter is going places. He has a good offer from News 24x7. I have wished him luck and am letting him move on.'

I was definitely not one of Rajan's pet reporters. As he congratulated me, his expression said it all; he was wondering how I got the opportunity with News 24x7.

I wanted to tell him that spotting talent was not a talent he had.

Rajeev supported me till my last day. He offered that he could waive off my notice period if I wanted to go off on a holiday before I joined my new job. So it was agreed that I would have to serve just a fortnight's notice.

I had been really lucky to have him as my first boss.

8

Stint with a Magazine

The HR department at News 24x7 informed us that their new office would be ready only after a month and we were expected to start work 15 days after that. This meant that I had 45 days for myself; I could either go on a holiday or do some freelancing. Being a workaholic I chose the latter.

Friends at a popular gossip magazine *GlamStruck* knew that I was good at making pages. The magazine apparently never hired full-time staff but only took freelancers for designing and page making. The only full-time employees were the reporters.

I agreed because they promised to pay me well—Rs 1000 per day, which was not bad at all. The editor was Tanya Joshi. She was known to jog at Marine Drive in the morning, work on the magazine during the day and hobnob at film parties in the night. She was a big name in the industry and at any given point of time could pick up the phone and call any top actor. Most of them would do anything to be on the cover. She was a shrewd boss and worked with a no-nonsense attitude. Her policy was simple—when you play, you play and when you work, you just work. Once your work was done no one would call you or try to contact you; that was her rule and everyone followed it strictly.

When I joined, I was the only boy in the team; the reporting team was an all-girls team and the other person who made the pages, was also a girl—she only worked on the ads and I worked on the articles.

I had no idea what I was getting into. Some friends had warned me, 'Dude, designing for a magazine is a different ball game altogether. It's not just adjusting columns and rows like you did at *The News*.'

I thought how different could it be. Above all, they were paying me good money, so I wouldn't mind working hard. I joined on a Monday. Since it was the first day of the week, there was full attendance. I was chatting with the reporters when the editor, Tanya, walked in. She looked stressed and angry.

Everyone stood up and said in unison, 'Good morning ma'am.'

She snapped, 'How can I have a good morning, girls? Who went for Shilpa Khanna's photoshoot yesterday?'

One girl stepped forward and I could tell that she was scared.

Shilpa Khanna was an upcoming actress who had a few hits, but the news for the magazine was that she was having an affair with the A-list actor, Sanjay Grover.

Tanya continued, 'I got the photos last night on email. What the hell is wrong with Shilpa's boobs? Come on girls! Didn't anyone notice anything?'

She took out blown up shots of Shilpa's swimsuit photos from a big envelope, 'Just look at them.'

'Oh yeah!' said one of the girls. Everyone was staring at them, so I did the same. The twin assets seemed fine to me! I wondered what the fuss was all about.

Tanya looked at me, 'Are you the new page designer?'

'Umm…yes ma'am. Raghu,' I fumbled and then smiled.

'Raghu, before you work on anything else, fix Shilpa's boobs. Come and show it to me once you are done.'

She looked at the reporter who had been present at the shoot and said, 'Call Shilpa and tell her that we would have to work on her boobs in post production. Make sure she doesn't have a problem,' and then added as an afterthought, 'Anyway, they are quite ugly so she should only be happy if we are working on them.'

Now, this was a culture shock! I came from a newspaper where we had to think twice before putting a photo of an actress showing her cleavage. And cut to this, where I would now have to photoshop someone's boobs before it got printed.

But what was wrong with them?

The only girl I could put this question to was Geetanjali, who had got me this job. I felt extremely awkward but I had to ask before I got down to my work.

'Hey Geet! You have a minute?'

She looked at me and understood my quandary. Laughing aloud, she asked, 'Were you scandalised?'

'Now you have to fix the boobs. I want to see what you do to them.' She said finally, trying to be serious, although I could still hear the laughter in her voice.

'It's not funny Geet! I have never done this before. I thought I had to design the pages. This is a totally different game *yaar*!'

She burst out laughing again.

'Geet, please help me…please,' I pleaded.

She finally agreed and I took her to the computer where pages were designed. I opened the images and zoomed in on…*them*.

'What's wrong with them?' I asked in complete confusion.

Geetanjali by now had doubled up in laughter. She was obviously used to all this and she knew that I was in a spot. Her mirth was infectious. Soon other reporters joined her in making fun of my predicament.

Finally between fits of laughter, she managed to ask, 'Look at them Raghu… Don't you think there is anything… wrong with them?'

I stared at the picture and then at Geetanjali…and back again. I didn't have the answer.

'The left one is looking smaller *na*!' She pointed out, 'Are you blind?'

'Really?' I stared again but didn't notice any difference in size.

I hadn't been this embarrassed in a very long time—officially discussing the size of boobs, that too with a girl, was definitely not how I had expected my first day of freelancing career to start.

Geetanjali was however feeling none of the awkwardness that I was experiencing. She casually advised, 'Push it slightly up and make it the same size as the right one. Make sure it doesn't look disfigured.'

I got to work immediately. After spending almost half a day on Shilpa's boobs, I managed to make them the same size.

Phew!

We took the prints to Tanya's cabin. She stared at them for five minutes, viewing the prints from various angles. She finally looked at me and said, 'Young man, you are good! Shilpa owes you a lot I must say. They look sexy now. This is our cover and men would be ogling at it once it hits the stands.'

She then asked the reporter to scan it and send it to Shilpa, 'Tell her that Tanya has approved of them, so she won't cause trouble. And honestly, she should be grateful to us.'

Shilpa's first reaction was that of protest. But when she was told that Tanya would go ahead with the *new shape*, there was little that the young starlet could do.

The day was over and I had passed my first test with flying colours.

At dinner, Reena asked me what kind of work I did with the magazine. I didn't have the guts to tell them what I had done that day.

'Just page designing. There were some swimsuit photos of Shilpa Khanna and I had to put them on the page and adjust text around them,' I said, trying to sound casual.

'Oh ho! So you saw swimsuit photos closely,' she said, pulling my leg, '*Aur kya chahiye* Raghu? (What more do you want Raghu?)'

Little did she know what I had actually done.

In the next few days I worked on boobs, butts, waist, hair and almost every other body part. And…I also fixed the biceps for men!

I wanted to share Shilpa's boob story with someone, for the sheer horror it had invoked in me. I finally got the opportunity when I met Rajeev for coffee. 'Dude, are you serious this is what magazines do? I always knew that they airbrush the hair and complexion. But shaping boobs is a bit too much,' Rajeev spoke out.

'On the first day, when I had to fix the boobs, I couldn't even figure what was wrong with them. The entire female staff was staring at them.'

Rajeev could not stop laughing, 'So what did you do?'

'I also stared at them. What else could I do?'

'This is hilarious!'

'After that, Geetanjali told me that the left one is small, so I had to keep staring at them again to figure this out for myself. And then make them the same size and shape,' I said, realising the humour behind the whole episode for the first time.

We just could not stop laughing. The girls at the next table stared at us, probably thinking that we were some perverts because they heard the word *boobs* several times.

Soon the magazine was on the stands. I saw it at a newspaper stall on my way back from work. I smiled to myself and brought some change out of my pocket to buy a copy.

When I took it home Reena snatched it from me. Her first reaction was, 'Oh my God! Shilpa looks hot. Wish I had a body like she does.'

As my sister stared at the cover, how I wished I could tell her that this body had been shaped by none other than her own brother!

Thanks to the magazine experience, I was now going to look at magazine covers differently; I don't think I would ever believe that any of the bodies on the covers were real, even if they were.

I worked for about a month and then I took 15 days off to just relax at home. I knew that once I started work with the news channel, life would be hectic. I didn't know when I would get my next break.

9

Learning the Ropes

I joined News 24x7. At the same time, several of my friends joined other channels like Planet and Khabar TV, but none of us got any formal training to face the camera, apart from a few drills here and there. Only after joining and starting work did I realise that writing for TV was different from writing for a newspaper. One had to keep the scripts short; a news story was usually for over a minute and less than two minutes, unless it was a special story.

I remember when the channel had not even gone on air, Aishwarya Rai had twisted her ankle in Nashik during the shoot of the film *Khakee*.

My boss came up to me and said, 'Go to Nashik and cover it. We will do some *phoners* with you. Then come back and file a story.'

'Really? We are not even on air and they are far away from Nashik. Where will the story air?' I asked in surprise.

'Get out of my face,' my boss snapped. 'Cover it. You are getting a chance to learn before we go on air,' saying so he left.

I didn't know anything; leave alone a '*phoner*.'

My cameraman, Andy, taught me a few things on the way; he basically gave me an idea about what was expected of me and how the whole thing was going to work.

On the way to Nashik we stopped at a *dhaba* for lunch.

Andy wondered why the channel was sending out untrained reporters on the field. He said, 'They have hired you guys from the print media. Tell your bosses that they have to train you first. The electronic media is *not* a cakewalk.'

'Well, Andy, I am new here too. I don't know how to approach the bosses. The reporters who have been hired don't even know each other, let alone share camaraderie.'

After a few hours we reached Nashik. Finding the shoot location was a task. We contacted some local reporters who had reported on Aishwarya's injury. They gave me a rough idea on where the film unit would be and also information on the hotel where the cast and crew were staying. We first went to the hotel. I met director Rajkumar Santoshi in the lobby and he was more than happy to have News 24x7 on the sets. He knew the brand but didn't know that we were not on air yet, and I didn't bother telling him that, because he would have then asked me why we were bothering to do the story.

I got him to talk on camera about Aishwarya's health. Then I called up my boss and updated him. He asked some anchors to do dummy phoners with me.

Andy said, 'Just answer the questions simply, the way you talk and be clear. Just don't think it's a phoner.' Thanks to Andy it all went off well.

I called up my boss again to inform him that I had got a health update on Aishwarya and had done some phoners, so could I return to Mumbai?'

'Not till you get Aishwarya Rai, my friend,' he said curtly and hung up.

I gathered courage and approached Rajkumar Santoshi once again, 'Sir, do you think I could get the opportunity to interview Aishwarya*ji*?'

He said I should ask the producer Keshu Ramsay. I found him at another location and when asked, he said it was okay if she was willing to talk.

No one was committing. It was after all my work!

Andy was sympathetic, 'Let's just go to her directly. There is no other way.'

We reached the sets, where we saw a big white vanity van. A paper stuck on the door said *Aishwarya Rai.* Some people were waiting outside, who we realised were members of her staff. We introduced ourselves and told them that we had spoken to the producer and the director and they both were okay with us doing a story from the set. We wanted to speak to Aishwarya.

One of them entered the van, and we assumed it was to seek her permission. We decided to wait…and waited… and waited. After more than 20 minutes he returned, saying, 'Madam *aapko bula rahi hai* camera *ke bina.* (Madam is calling you but without the camera.)'

I knocked and entered the plush interiors of the van. Contrary to the heat outside, the van was cold, and comfortably so.

I couldn't wait to get a glimpse of the gorgeous Miss World; had seen her only in photographs—never got the opportunity to interview her.

She welcomed me warmly, 'You have come all the way from Mumbai?'

I was awestruck!

I had to be professional with my approach since I represented a news channel, but only I knew that I was as excited as a fan.

'Yes, the news of you hurting yourself on a film set has got a lot of your fans worried.'

'How sweet! But I am not doing any interviews now. This leg injury is bad and there is a lot of work. I promise to do an interview with you once I am back in Mumbai.'

When an actor refuses, sometimes it is best to step back and let them have their way to build a long-term relationship. Of course, if it was breaking news I would pursue it more. But this was far from it and we were not even on air.

I told Andy what happened inside the van and then called my boss and informed him. 'It's okay Raghu, come back, but if we were on air, then I wouldn't let you come back without her interview.' I could sense this was a kind of warning, probably because I had asked him earlier if I could come back.

Next morning when I knocked at the editor's glass door, he announced, 'Raghu, you missed the camera training yesterday. Go and sit in the batch that's on now.'

I rushed to the room where the training class was being held and learnt that I had missed over an hour of this two-hour training.

Sayeed, a senior cameraman, was conducting the class. He noticed me walking in late and promised to help me with some of the things I had missed. During the class, we were told that we have to always help the cameraman; if he was lifting the camera bag then the reporter had to lift the tripod—this was the most important rule to work as a team.

Next day I had to cover a press conference and my cameraman for the day was Sayeed. When it was time to leave, I remembered the lesson from the previous day; since he was carrying the camera bag, I lifted the tripod.

'I will manage, don't worry,' saying so he took it from me. 'That was just theoretical information. In reality, this is the cameraman's job. Don't repeat this to anyone. You are like my friend so I am telling you.'

I insisted but he didn't let me carry the tripod or the camera bag.

When we returned to the office, once again I tried to take the tripod out of the car but he said he would manage. 'You go ahead and file your story,' he told me and I went ahead to my workstation.

It so happened that the production head and my editor walked out and saw him carry the camera bag and the tripod. They asked him who the reporter was who he had accompanied and why he was not helping out.

Sayeed replied, '*Arre,* this is how the young reporters are. Nobody is willing to help the cameraman.'

I was summoned.

The editor was scathing, 'Raghu, why is Sayeed carrying both the camera and the tripod? Couldn't you help him? You know how senior he is?'

I tried to say that I had offered help but was cut short before I could even begin.

'Raghu, just take it from him,' the editor reprimanded. 'And remember you have to always carry the tripod. You are not a star.'

I finally spoke out, 'But sir, I had asked Sayeed if I could carry it, he had said no.'

'Don't ask. Just do it,' the editor said and left.

I noticed that Sayeed has a smirk on his face. I couldn't believe what had just happened. I failed to understand why a senior person like Sayeed did that, why did he make me look like the bad one?

I confronted him, 'Sayeed, didn't I offer to help? Why didn't you say so?'

He just laughed and walked away without answering.

The receptionist who had been watching all this drama looked at me and said, 'Welcome to the bitch fest! You will learn the ropes soon. Don't take much tension over this. These things keep happening.'

I talked to some reporters after a few days and warned them to be cautious about Sayeed. Aparna, a new recruit like me, shared something far more worse, 'He has been sending me weird messages late in the night.'

'What do you mean by weird messages?' one of us asked.

'One night, at around one, he sent a message saying, *Hey what u doing*? You know one of those messages we send to our close friends or maybe to our partners.'

'That's crazy!'

'I didn't reply to it, but that didn't stop him. He messaged again the next night saying, *Attitude haan! You looked pretty today. You will do very well here. If you need any help I will be one call away.* The next morning I just texted saying, *Thank You*. I didn't know what to say. Ass***e!'

'Oh God!'

'So creepy! I have decided that if he does it again, I will complain to either his boss or mine. I just won't tolerate this.'

Aparna was a pretty girl and an amazing person. She continued, 'I am used to all this. It happens in a lot of places but I just wait for people to back off. I have a boyfriend and even if I was single there was no way Sayeed would have a chance.'

As luck would have it, the next day Aparna was assigned a shoot with Sayeed. I was sure he had manipulated this. Once they were back, I saw Aparna walking straight to the editor's cabin, which was right opposite my desk. They spoke for a long time and I could see, through the glass door, that she was very animated. I could sense that she was angry.

Mr Kamble, the editor, soon picked up the phone and was talking to someone while Aparna, looked towards the door and saw me staring at her. She stared at me and nodded and I understood that it was about Sayeed. I wondered what he had done now that made her walk straight up to the editor to complain. Kamble and Aparna walked to the first floor where the production team worked; where Sayeed's boss could be found.

I had no idea what was happening but I couldn't wait for Aparna to get back. When she did I went up to her. There weren't that many people in the newsroom as it was a Saturday. Aparna didn't want to talk about it and said she will tell me after office. She was still not in a good mood. At about 6 p.m. she shut her computer, lifted her shoulder bag and looked at me as if to say, 'Let's step out.'

As we walked throught the corridor, she asked, 'Aren't you leaving? There is no work right?'

'Yeah! There is nothing, but I am the only reporter on duty till 9 p.m. So, can't leave in case something turns up.'

We walked up to the tea stall at the end of the road for a cup of tea.

'So what the hell happened?' I asked her, unable to quell my curiosity anymore.

'Same shit man! We were on our way for a shoot. You know we get these indica cars, so he kept the big camera bag on the front seat. So it was obvious that both of us would sit in the rear seat. And he started hitting on me.'

'What did he do?'

'First he started the topic by saying how he had waited for my message the first night and that he couldn't sleep because I didn't reply.'

'Oh!'

'Yeah, I just changed the topic and then he just put his hand on my hand. I just took away my hand and snapped at him, "Sayeed stop it! Don't ever touch me and don't send me messages." But that too didn't stop him. He thought I was upset, so he justified his thought by giving me a hug! I just told the driver to stop the car there and then. He immediately apologised and we went ahead for the assignment. It was so difficult to shoot with him after that because I had to talk to him; I had to tell him what shots I needed. He just acted difficult and kept telling me how the shot I wanted was not possible.

'I walked up and told the boss everything. He took me to Sayeed's boss and we complained. The HR manager was called and they are taking action against him. He will not be able to come to work till they take a final decision on my complaint. I hate this. This is what I didn't want in this new work place.'

'Yeah I know what you mean but it is not your fault. He had to be checked. Really sad because he has been with this company for a decade now.'

When she finally took a cab and headed home, I realised that I had never seen Aparna so upset before.

I returned to the office to realise that the word had spread because the driver had told other drivers what had happened in the car and they in turn told the other reporters and cameramen who they knew well. Word spreads like wildfire in the media. Andy called me to check what had happened because he knew that I was working today.

He was shocked when I told him everything. 'These are the people who create a bad name for cameramen. They should just throw him out. Ridiculous behaviour.'

He told me that Sayeed had done something similar in the past and had been let off with a warning.

I reached home and shared the office goss with mom and Reena.

'Oh my God! What a jerk,' Reena responded.

Mom said, '*Beta*, you stay away from him.'

Reena and I look at each other and burst out laughing.

'Ya Raghu... What if...he hits on you...or holds your hand in the car,' Reena said between spurts of laughter.

I wrapped up my day after watching the popular English comedy *Friends* on TV.

Next morning, my phone rang as I was reading the newspaper and having breakfast.

'Reena, please pass the phone,' I yelled out to my sister.

'Hey! It's Aparna. Pick up, pick up,' Reena said as she handed over the phone.

Aparna told me that Sayeed had been sacked. The editor had called to tell her that she could now come to work without any hesitation as Sayeed did not work with the channel anymore; they had dismissed him without notice for his unprofessional behaviour. The editor had apologised on behalf of the company.

Reena had been staring at me throughout, so, I had to give her an immediate update. 'Good! This should happen to men who make women uncomfortable,' she responded emphatically.

Andy called me next with the same update. I told him that I already knew. '*Acha hua*,' he kept saying.

For several days after this, Sayeed was the main topic of conversation in the office. Even the other channels came to know of this episode as he was a senior cameraman. The speculation was rife that he would find it difficult to get work with other channels.

For us novices, this was an eye-opener to the TV media industry that we had joined.

10

Newsroom Politics

The personal experiences with senior cameraman Sayeed made me wary of my co-workers; I didn't trust anyone at my new workplace. It took me a few months and many shoots before I warmed up to cameraman Andy. We became friends and he took the place that Mohan Bhai had occupied while I was in the print media.

What I learnt over a period of time was that it was important to get along with a few cameramen and work exclusively with them on assignments. This rapport was also important for every cameraman, who would have their favourite set of reporters. We tried to ensure that for most projects we got this reporter-cameraman combination right.

I had my contacts in the film industry, from my days in the print media, and now with a brand like News 24x7 behind me, I started making inroads in the film world. I got along with all the important people in Bollywood. In less than six months the biggest stars started calling me directly.

This however didn't go down well with Shereen, a film reporter, who had been working with News 24x7 since the time it was just a cable TV network. Aware of her good looks, she would ensure that her derrière and cleavage got her the necessary attention. Her hair and make-up were always perfect, even on the days she just sat at her desk. She even claimed that when she couldn't find the right eyeliner or the perfect lip colour to go with her mood, she chose not to come for work; and she did not hesitate to talk about this. Truth be told, Shereen was very close to the owners of the channel and hence received a lot of perks along with a hefty salary.

When all the big interviews started coming to me, Shereen could not accept it graciously, more so as she was technically my senior.

In the business of news, gossip always manages to reach where it perhaps ought not to; I got to know that Shereen had been telling the colleagues she was friendly with, that she would cut me to size some day and that I would quit like the others before me.

In the past, quite a few people had quit because of Shereen's attitude. She would either rile them till they reacted or she seemed to have a vendetta against them; either way, the reporter would quit when he/she could not take it anymore. She spared no one. The office boys were scared of her; one call from her extension and the boys would leave everything aside to prepare her coffee and make sure it reached her desk in less than five minutes. The joke in the office was that if you saw an office boy rushing like the devil was at his heels, you just knew it had to be because of Shereen.

There is always a dull period, during the year, when there are no events in town; when actors are either travelling abroad for holidays or shows or out of the city for film shoots. The entertainment shows are filled with run-of-the-mill desk stories, countdown songs and similar events. It is during this period that Shereen called me to her desk one day.

'Since we have a lot of time on hand now, why don't you follow the story of legendary actor Akbar Ali's love affair?'

'Love affair? But isn't he married?' I asked in surprise.

'He is and has a very clean image here in Bollywood, but he recently slept with a Hollywood script writer at his farmhouse. She is a regular visitor there over the weekends. Do you get what I am saying?'

'Yes, but don't you know the family very well?'

'Yes I do and that's the reason I can get you all the information, but I can't do the story myself. I don't want to burn the bridges. They don't know you from Adam; you are a newbie and therefore the best person to do this. If you manage to tarnish Akbar Ali's holier than thou image, you will be a famous reporter. And the best part is that it's all true, darling! Not just gossip!'

'Yeah! Let me think about it and get back to you,' I said, somewhat wary of why Shereen would pass on a good lead to me.

'Let me know soon or else I will pass it on to someone who wants to grow in this industry,' she threw the obvious taunt at me.

There was a lot of thinking to do for this so called *golden opportunity* as she called it. A story served on a platter with all the information from someone close to the family and that too from someone who certainly could not be considered as among my well-wishers! Furthermore, what was troubling me was that if Shereen was close to the family why would she want to bring Akbar Ali down? Another problem was that such stories couldn't be discussed with anyone, because if the word spread, someone else might do the story.

I thought the best person who could advise me on this would be Rajeev.

He did not answer his mobile. I tried his number a couple of times before I called his residence landline. Rajeev's mother answered.

'Hi Aunty, this is Raghu.'

She was affable as usual, 'How are you doing? We see you on News 24x7 and are very proud of you.'

'Thanks aunty! Keep watching and please give me your feedback whenever you can.'

'Sure! You want to speak to Rajeev but he is out of the country. He is back next week.'

I was very disappointed. 'Has he gone on work?' I asked.

'Yes, he has gone for some interviews with Hollywood stars; that's what he told me.'

I disconnected the call but only after promising her that I would drop by sometime soon.

Damn! My only good advisor was not available. I knew that Shereen was waiting for my answer. She didn't look too happy when I had asked for some time to think about it. I now told myself that if I did not take up the assignment she would surely pass it onto someone else—it could be an opportunity missed. She might go to my seniors and complain about me saying that I did not follow up on the lead she had offered.

The next morning, Shereen walked up to me before going to her cubicle, 'So you are doing the story right? I have some more update for you.'

For some reason she was determined that I do the story. That should have set the alarm bells ringing. But I threw caution to the winds. 'Screw it!' I told myself, 'The worst scenario would be one bad story coming out of all this; out of the many stories that we do regularly. And if it wasn't a great one it would go unnoticed.'

I took down all the information she had for me, including the address of the farmhouse and the day the *other woman* in Akbar Ali's life would be visiting the farm.

At the end of the day, while leaving, Shereen asked me if I wanted to join her for a spin in her new car. We walked out and she asked the driver to go home. We both sat in her BMW and she sped away from the office.

It was quite late in the night and she entered one of the quieter lanes in the neighbourhood. It primarily had banks and government offices and was known to get desolate by late evening.

'Nice car!' I said, attempting to start a conversation. She had been unusually quiet. What happened next was something I had never imagined. Shereen brought the car to a halt, took off her seat belt and came close to me.

Before I knew it, we were kissing. The long-drawn kisses soon turned into something more intimate. And then… just as suddenly as it had started… we stopped.

Oh My God! Wow! I told myself, feeling the blood rush to all parts of my body. Shereen appeared quite non-plussed. She put on her seat belt, started the car and before I knew it I was at the office gate.

She waited, without a word again, as if waiting for me to step out of the car, which I did after 10 confusing seconds.

As I shut the door, she said, 'Raghu, we could do this more often. But don't fall in love with me. Bye.' She gave me an enigmatic smile and drove off.

I couldn't believe what had just happened. I *kissed* Shereen Luthra! I mean she kissed me! Whatever! We kissed! It was wrong… Seemed right! Who the hell cared! And we could do this more often, she had said. Wow! I just couldn't stop thinking about it and the smile on my face just wouldn't go away.

I will do the story so well that she will be completely impressed, I told myself. I soon got cracking on the lead. I went to Ali's film set the day media was invited to cover the shooting of a song sequence for his next film *Wafaa*.

I took the opportunity to casually bring up Saira's name with Akbar Ali's make-up man and spot boy.

'Saira madam *toh sahab ki bahaut achi dost hai. Woh to set pe kai baar aati hai. Aap jaante hain unko?* (Saira Madam is a good friend of Sahab. She comes to the sets quite often. Do you know her?)'

I told them that I was acquainted with her. Excited that Shereen's lead was bang on, I tried to get more information from them; like when did she visit the sets.

What I gathered was that every alternate day she came to the sets just before pack-up and then the two left together in the same car.

So I decided to visit the next day without a voice recorder or a cameraman; just like a fan and wander around, keeping an eye from a distance. Pack-up time was around nine in the evening and an hour before that a black Honda Accord arrived and parked right next to Akbar's van. His staff opened the door of her car and she stepped out and rushed into his vanity van. I could just see that she was tall and wearing a red dress, with her hair neatly done up; but couldn't see her face.

Next morning I reached office early, waiting eagerly to update Shereen. I saw her at the door and shouted, 'Guess what?'

'You seem excited, babe?' She asked me with a smile as she placed her bag on the desk and pulled up a chair.

'You were right about Saira. I saw her yesterday. She came to meet Akbar just as they were packing up after the shoot at Mehboob Studios. I am told this happens every alternate day.'

'I told you darling. Just get the story before someone else finds out about it. Don't discuss it with too many people,' she whispered and touched my hand and gave me a naughty smile, as if to indicate that we were now a team.

I refused to move my hand as she tried to pull it away and she came close to my ear and whispered, 'We are in the office Raghu.'

Then she smiled and pushed back her chair.

I decided to update her on my plans.

'Tomorrow is Saturday and I am taking Andy to the farmhouse. We will wait at a distance. All I need are some good shots; if we can get just one glimpse of Akbar and Saira together then my story is done. We will just run these as nobody is going to give me a confirmation on camera, right?' I checked with her.

'Good idea,' she encouraged. 'When you get some shots of them… together, get some reactions from the general public before sending this to the press. It is anyway a gossipy piece so play it the best way you can.'

'That's a good idea,' I was thrilled at her encouragement.

Next day Andy and I drove to Panvel to Akbar's farmhouse. We reached by 10 a.m. and parked ourselves at a distance. Andy had taken a zoom lens so that we could shoot from a distance. We had also carried stuff to eat, as it could be a long wait.

Andy asked me, 'Raghu, are you sure about this story?'

I was surprised at his query and responded with confidence, 'Yes, Shereen has given me the lead. And I checked with his staff and even saw her visiting the sets. Now if she is a friend why would she visit him every other day before pack-up and why would they always leave together? They don't go to Akbar's house. Why do they come to this farmhouse? Come on Andy, I am sure you can see the obvious.'

'You maybe right but why is that Dracula helping you?'

'Dracula? What do you mean?'

'All the cameramen refer to Shereen as Dracula. Don't tell her that,' Andy responded.

As I burst out laughing, Andy asked, 'If it's such a big Bollywood story of a top actor then why is *she* not doing it?'

'Dracula... I mean Shereen, is close to Akbar and obviously she doesn't want to burn her bridges. I don't know Akbar at all. So it makes sense. But why does everyone hate her so much?'

'Oh! She has slept with the entire world to get her work done. She will not think twice about manipulating somebody to suit herself. You will get to know with time. Just make sure you script the story carefully.'

'Don't worry!'

At around 2 p.m. we sent the driver to get us some *vada pav* and then we just waited under a tree with the camera.

In about 20 minutes our driver came back in a rush saying that the black Honda Accord had entered the farmhouse from the back gate. We realised that they would also leave from the same gate. We jumped into our car and parked where we could get a clear view of the back gate.

There was no one there; not even a watchman. We just waited in the silence surrounding us. The bungalow was located a little away from the main road. We had realised that the bungalows in the vicinity were all unoccupied; that probably accounted for the silence.

Andy suddenly spotted Akbar and Saira on the terrace. But he couldn't get a clear shot of their faces. Asking the driver to wait in the car, in case we needed to make a quick getaway, Andy and I walked into the bushes in search of a vantage point to film the two together. He finally found a tree that he could climb.

'You stay closeby and keep an eye on possible interruptions,' Andy instructed me as he looked into his viewfinder.

'Can you see anything?' I asked him, a notch loudly at the prospect of this *breaking news*.

'Shhh! I can see everything. They are having coffee and talking as they walk around the terrace,' Andy responded, focussing his camera.

After 10 minutes he jumped down. 'Raghu I have the shots. We must get out of here soon. This is private property and we could be handed over to the cops, if caught. I will shoot the bungalow from a distance.'

I needed more spice for the story, 'Okay, how about this? We wait till the black car leaves the premises and take a couple of shots of that. If we are lucky we might get some of her.'

Andy agreed and as we walked up to the car, he pointed out, 'What will you write about these visuals? They are just having coffee and talking. Doesn't prove anything. If we had seen them kissing or some such thing then you would have got a real story. But this means nothing.'

'Don't worry. I will manage the story.'

We again waited, this time for Saira's car to leave the bungalow. It was a long wait. Finally, the car left at 8 p.m. It was not too difficult for Andy to film the car as we were parked at the perfect point.

Back home, I shared the story with my sister and made her promise that she wouldn't discuss it with anyone, till my story went on air.

I had trouble falling asleep that night. The excitement at having achieved something big kept me awake. Andy and I had managed to pull off something great. Even as I tried to sleep, I told myself what a sick place this industry was! Akbar Ali had everything—money, fame, a loving wife, fans, hit movies—but he had to cheat on his wife.

The more I learnt about this industry, the more I told myself… I hate Bollywood.

11

My First Exposé… Exposed!

Next morning I was in the office early. Andy and I stepped out and visited a mall nearby to talk to general public about Akbar Ali's extra-marital affair. We spoke to young college students who were hanging around in groups; from previous experiences we knew that the young college crowd was always ready to talk on camera. They are keen to see themselves on television. And the interaction always ended with '*Kab aaega? Kaunse channel pe?* (When will it be aired? On which channel?)'

I first told them how Akbar Ali was cheating on his wife and we had the first visuals of the lady he was having an affair with. We then showed them some of the visuals we had on camera. The reaction was just as we had expected.

Most of them reacted saying they didn't expect this from their favourite actor. Job done, I rushed back to the office, logged the tapes and wrote my script.

It ran thus…

Anchor: And now it's time for some Bollywood gossip. Hold your hearts ladies, we have some news about your favourite star Akbar Ali. The actor, it has been discovered, is seeing another mystery lady. Here is more from our reporter Raghu Kumar who visited the actor's panvel farmhouse…

Voice-over One: 8 p.m. Akbar Ali's farmhouse in Panvel. A black Honda Accord drives out of the bungalow and zooms on to the highway. Let's see what happened earlier in the day. (Ten second shot of them having coffee on the terrace.)

Vox pop one (Girl with glasses): Oh my God! I can't believe it. Akbar with another woman. He is a youth icon. How can he do this?

Voice-over Two: The lady's name is Saira and she not only visits his film set regularly, but they are seen leaving together, every alternate day, just before the unit packs up. Ali's staff confirmed this off camera.

Vox pop two: (Girl in red top): I really didn't expect Akbar Ali to be like that. But then film actors are known for doing such things. It's his choice.

Vox pop three: (Boy in gray shirt): He is such a popular actor. Why did he have to do this?

PTC (At a theatre standing in front of his poster): Akbar Ali has amassed a huge fan following with his films. But his fans are clearly not amused with this slice from his life. Will this now start affecting the box-office numbers? We will just have to wait and watch. This is Raghu Kumar, News 24x7, Mumbai.

I showed the script to Shereen and she said that it was perfect. I then sent it to the copy editor for checking.

There are some copy editors who change the entire story; they ask a number of questions to improve the copy. And that sometimes changes the entire spin of the story and the peg changes. While the other category of copy editors only correct the grammatical errors, if any. My story landed with Carol who trusted my take on a news piece and hence she just made some grammatical corrections.

The script was ready, the bytes and shots were logged which meant we were ready to edit.

The usual practice is for the Mumbai Bureau to send a day plan to the head office, at the end of the day. Since there was nothing much happening in the city, my story was third from the top, which meant it would not only be played on our entertainment shows but will also be a part of the general news wheel.

I sat in late for the edit with one of the best editors. During the tea break the video editor asked me, 'It's a great story boss! How did you know that Saira visited his farmhouse?'

I responded with aplomb, 'Got a tip from a source, then Andy and I parked ourselves near the farmhouse and the bird got trapped…in our camera.'

We shared a hearty laugh and went back to the edit.

The editor used some latest hit numbers of Akbar Ali for the story; the popular song, 'Dhokebaaz…' from his last release, was the perfect background score. I knew that once this was telecast I would be catapulted into the big league.

After the edit I walked over to Shereen who was working late. 'Shereen, I want to thank you for this. It's such a huge story. Thank you very much.'

'Raghu you are a darling…you deserve it,' she said and hugged me.

I didn't want to disturb her by chitchatting as she had obviously stayed back for work. I headed back to my desk, made sure the story was uplinked to Delhi and once that was done I mailed my script to the desk in Delhi and then left for the day.

Exhausted…but satisfied.

I did expect a lot of feedback so I woke up at 8 a.m. to see the story being played back to back—8 a.m., 9 a.m, 10 a.m, and so on.

And then the calls began—the first were other reporters, most of them telling me how their bosses were pressurising them to go behind this story. And then there was a call from my Mumbai Bureau head, Anil Kamble, 'Raghu, great one!'

'Thank you sir.'

'Kranti called to say that it's a great story from Bollywood and that we should do more stories like this. So don't get roped into covering daily events. There is a real reporter in you.'

I was in seventh heaven, 'Thank you so much sir, thank you.'

I hung up and ran to my mom and sister to give them the good news. 'My story is a hit! My story is a hit! Kranti also liked it. Yay!'

I walked into office around noon and almost everyone came forward to greet me. Anil Kamble called me to his desk and ordered a coffee as we chatted. This had never happened before.

I was eager to share the joy of this success with Shereen, but she wasn't around. I learnt that she had been working late and had seen the story on the edit machine before leaving.

Throughout the day I got calls and text messages for my story. The day zoomed past; I did nothing but walked around or surfed the net. I was, after all, the star reporter of the day. News 24x7 was running its best story, thanks to yours truly, I told myself.

Back home in the evening, as I had dinner with family, I told my mom and sister that this had been one of the most awesome days in my professional career. As I hit the bed, my mind was still full of all the compliments that I had received throughout the day. I had no idea what the next day held in store for me.

I woke up to the sound of my phone ringing. It was 9 a.m. and Anil Kamble was on the line.

'Rush to office now. I want you here as soon as possible. Your story is all wrong. We are in deep trouble because of you. Akbar Ali has sued our channel. You have no idea what you have done.'

I sat there in stunned silence; unable to respond to what I had just heard. So the party was over, maybe my career too…

My mom and sister were anxious to see me speeding through the house to get ready. But I just couldn't explain anything to them. I had to reach the office soon.

Several thoughts raced through my mind as I made my way: Would I be sacked as I reached office? What if the legal case was only against me as the reporter? I didn't have the means to fight a legal battle against Akbar Ali. But more importantly, how could Shereen's tip be wrong?

I entered the office and the entire floor went quiet; pin-drop silence as against the usual buzz of the newsroom—as opposed to the congratulatory wishes that had come my way yesterday, today the occupants of the room just stared at me. Some spoke in hushed tones. The peon was the only one who spoke to me, informing me that Kamble was very angry and had been on the phone forever.

'What research did you do on this story? Who told you all this?' Kamble threw at me, without a preamble.

'Sir, I got the shots and…the lead…the lead was given by Shereen,' I fumbled.

'What! Shereen gave you this story?'

'Yes sir! She told me she couldn't do the story herself because she was close to Ali...so...she wanted me to do it.'

Kamble immediately dialled Shereen from his cell phone.

'Shereen, I know you are on leave from today, but I need to speak to you for five minutes.'

He then put the phone on loudspeaker and asked her, 'Is it true that you gave Raghu the lead for the Akbar Ali story?'

Shereen responded immediately, 'What? Me? Of course not. What rubbish.'

I was stunned!

But then I recovered realising that I had to find out what was going on, 'Shereen, why are you lying? You know you gave me the lead. Just say it man.'

Shereen had probably expected that a newbee like me would never challenge her, so she now screeched over the phone, 'Don't believe him Anil. Raghu is just trying to cover his ass. For some reason, best known to him, he wants me to get into trouble. This is ridiculous.'

Kamble disconnected the call, 'Why are you lying, Raghu? Tell me the real story behind this fake story of yours. Who gave you this lead?'

I could barely talk.

Kamble handed me the legal notice sent by Akbar Ali's lawyer, saying, 'It's a defamation case asking for a compensation of Rs 5 crore and an apology at 9 p.m. primetime. This has never happened since our launch. And the lady in your breaking story is Saira, a popular author who is writing Akbar's biography. Hence you have seen her wherever you have seen her. How could you just allege something like this? Our lawyers will be here in half an hour. Let's just tell them everything and see what they suggest.'

As I walked out of Kamble's office, I could sense that all eyes in the newsroom were on me. Some of the reporters came forward to console me. I failed to understand why Shereen would do this to me. Within 24 hours, my story, which was appreciated by all, had become a source of embarrassment for the channel—my bosses who had praised me for my work and spoke about my potential to be a great journalist were now doubting my credentials. How would I win back the trust I had lost today?

I had become the *story for the day*. How was I going to change that?

Andy took me to the tea stall outside, 'Didn't I tell you, something just didn't seem right?'

I did not really want to hear somebody say, *I told you so*, but I knew that Andy was a genuine well-wisher. So after sitting through a tirade in which he once again told me to watch out for Shereen, I headed back to the office, this time to meet the company lawyer.

I found myself seated with the legal team and Kamble in the conference room. Kamble came to the point directly, 'To be honest, it's our fault. We didn't pay attention to this story and let it go on air because, usually, Bollywood stories do not get that much attention.'

He continued, 'Raghu is a rookie reporter and as we know now, this was done after some really haphazard research work. Some stupid tip off and this bugger got excited and did the story. Anyway, now what do you suggest?'

The team of lawyers was from Veena Thadani Associates, one of the most reputed law firms in Mumbai.

The lawyers did not look as tensed as I had been feeling the whole day. One of them finally said, 'Just the usual! We will stand by our story; we had information that Ali was dating

Saira. Just because she is his biographer does not mean that nothing is happening between them. We will argue that the news is true according to our reporter's source and as per the law a journalist is not obligated to reveal his or her source. It's gossip anyway! We will handle it. Raghu might have to come to the court a couple of times before this is sorted out. But ensure that the issue is not discussed with anyone.'

Sounding relieved, Kamble said, 'Raghu is all yours, you can have him at the court whenever you want.'

I myself was not quite happy with the idea of visiting a court, but was glad that the company was going to stand by through this. I had thought I would just be abandoned.

After the meeting, Kamble called me to his cabin and offered me tea as he asked me to sit. I did not care much for the tea but was relieved to see that he looked visibly relaxed; very different from my earlier visit to his office.

'I can't tell you how sorry I am sir,' I offered, 'I had no idea...'

'Listen! You are a good guy and I still say that you are a good reporter. This time you were taken for a ride. I don't know why! But I do know that this is not the first time Shereen has done something like this. She has done this to reporters in the past, who then quit their job later. See, there is no proof that she gave you the tip. It appears as though you are just palming off this *faux pas* to her, for whatever reason.'

I was surprised at this revelation, 'Sir, you believe me, right?'

'Yes I do, but I am afraid I won't be able to do much about this mischief that Shereen had deliberately caused,' Kamble confessed.

'But why? She has been doing all this under your nose. Even if no one must feel bad for me, what she is doing is bad for the channel?'

'Now listen, Raghu. Firstly, you have no proof that she gave you this tip; it's your word against her. Secondly, she is close to the Mittal family, who own this channel and they will believe her. If you take it up, you might end up losing your job. You can gauge her association with the family from the fact that the last big party that they hosted at their private pad in Goa, Shereen was the only employee present. She has more shares in the company than I do. So, don't come in her way again and stay away from her, for your own good. I am telling you this as a well wisher, remember this and keep it to yourself.'

I had understood the scene and left his office after thanking him.

I decided to leave for the day; couldn't imagine hanging around after all that had happened today. Just then I came across Carol, who was walking into the office.

'Hey Raghu! I got an earful from Kamble because of your story today. He has warned me that from now onwards I should ask the reporters questions about their stories; not just copy edit. You know "Where have you got the lead from?" and "Can you vouch for it?" Now tell me *yaar*, is this the work of a copy editor?'

I only apologised to her and stepped out.

This must have been the worst day of my life. I was trying to climb the ladder of success step by step but thanks to Shereen I was now down in the dumps. The only good thing was that my bureau head knew that it was not my fault. But he must be thinking what a fool I was to have been duped so easily. Unfortunately, this will always be remembered as my story. What must Kranti think about me now, after praising me yesterday. I wish I hadn't been this gullible. I remembered the moment in Shereen's car and realised that it had all been a carefully thought out plan. Like a fool I had walked into the trap.

Just then my phone rang. An unknown number.

I picked up the phone reluctantly, praying that it was not somebody related to Ali, calling me to reprimand me for my story.

The voice on the other end however was a balm to my wounded self-esteem.

'Hey! Raghu, this is Rajeev. I am in London and this is my local number. What happened? I heard about some problem with your story.'

I was stunned. 'How did you find out? That too in London?'

'Some friends from my Mumbai office told me; they know you are my friend.'

'Ya man! I have had the worst day of my life,' I let out finally. 'I had a doubt about this lead so I called you also the other day. Your mom told me that you were travelling abroad. There was no one else I could go for advice. So I did the story and things got all screwed up. It was a trap.'

'Trap? Why would someone trap you?'

'I know who, but I don't know why, at least not yet. Shereen gave me a wrong tip and practically pushed me to do the story. Now she is denying that she gave me the lead.'

'But why would Shereen do that Raghu?' Rajeev sounded surprised. 'It doesn't make sense.'

'I want to just kill her. She has screwed me up so badly and for what I don't even know.'

'Okay, okay! Just calm down. It happens. I am back tomorrow. We can meet and talk at length.'

'Thank God! Yes, please make time and meet me as soon as you get here.'

Disconnecting the call I acknowledged to myself how relieved I already felt. Rajeev had more experience of this industry than I did. He would probably help me find an explanation to this experience with Shereen.

I reached home and hugged my mom, long enough for both her and my sister to guess that I was upset over something. So I told them all that had happened through the day; how things had changed from the day before when I was a star reporter.

Reena was furious, 'Shereen's a bitch! How could she do this?'

'Reena, mind your language!' Mom chastised her.

'I am sorry mom, but why did she do this to Raghu?'

Mom was her usual calm self, 'These are important lessons in life. There are good people and there are bad people. Clearly Shereen tried to pull you, a junior, down. I wish this had not happened but there is a lesson here… learn and move on.'

'Did your boss shout at you?'

'My immediate boss was nowhere in sight; probably on leave, I think. But the Bureau head, Kamble, has understood that I was trapped.'

'What! The Bureau head knows about it. So why is he not taking any action against Shereen?' Reena screeched.

I told them that Shereen was close to the Mittal family and that they would surely come to her defence if I made any kind of accusation.

Later, as we turned in for the night, I remembered that I had actually kissed her and thereby walked into a trap. What a fool I was!

I remembered the words of the receptionist, 'Welcome to the bitch fest.'

And all this because of a Bollywood story!

12

Lying Low

I took the following day off and just stayed at home. I didn't have the guts to go to the newsroom again, with all eyes staring at me. Most of them would be nice to my face, but I know what they would be thinking.

Andy called to check how I was doing, so did a few other journalist friends.

Rajeev called around four in the evening, 'Hi, I have just left the airport. Let's do dinner in Bandra.'

'Yes, that's a great idea. See you at around nine at Olive?'

'Done!'

I got there before time, as is my habit for all meetings; personal or professional.

Surprisingly, Rajeev reached five minutes before 9 p.m. which was unusual for him.

Rajeev had achieved a celebrity status soon after joining Channel Planet. His show was doing extremely well and had the highest TRPs across Indian TV shows. People recognised him almost everywhere.

At Olive, the manager gave us a table immediately and even pulled the chair out for us saying, 'Rajeev*ji*, I watch your show on Planet TV. You are doing an awesome job, I must say. We are glad to have you at our restaurant.'

Finally we sat down and were soon discussing my big goof up.

He was shocked to hear the details, 'I absolutely fail to understand why Shereen would do this to you. It's just crazy.' After a brief pause, he added, 'Jealousy could be a reason; you are doing well and making a name for yourself with the channel. Come to think of it, entertainment is her beat too.'

'Come on Rajeev. I am a junior and she is *The* Shereen! If she is insecure about me then that's just plain stupid. She wines and dines with the Mittals.'

'Raghu, just forget what happened. Just stay out of her way now onwards. Don't confront her and don't...'

I cut him short, 'If I don't confront her I will never find out why she did this.'

'That's not important. What is important is to bounce back and regain the respect you have lost in the eyes of your bosses. You have to work extra hard and just prove your worth. That's it.'

I did not like the idea of Shereen getting away with this, but I trusted Rajeev's judgement on how to best handle the situation.

'Will people ever forget this?' I wondered aloud.

'See Raghu, people inside the channels know this; outsiders don't. And everything is forgotten with time. Trust me! The people who know will eventually forget this. Thankfully, Akbar Ali has not gone to the media with this. There was nothing related to this in today's newspaper, which means it's over. Clearly, he too doesn't want to blow it up.'

We all knew that Akbar Ali had some reporters on his payroll, who wrote stories on things he wanted to publicise, but for some reason he too wanted this issue to die down.

It is only later, that I learnt, through Rajeev's friend, that Akbar was going through a rough patch in his marriage and did not want any of this gossip to blow up and affect his family.

After my dinner with Rajeev, I felt much better, because he was well respected in the industry. He had been around for years; long before I had stepped in. He knew and understood more about the place than I did. And I trusted him to give me the right advice.

On my way back I told myself that I would have to spring back to my feet. No more of avoiding people at work. I would be at work the next day.

In no time, I was back to covering events. Sometimes other reporters in the field would ask me about the Akbar Ali story but that too stopped after a few weeks.

I watched Shereen in the office. Obviously, we didn't talk to each other. She knew what she had done. At times, I wish I could tell everybody how we had kissed in her car, but that was not going to do me any good. So I lived by the advice given by Rajeev and some other friends; just stayed out of her way.

I had learnt my lesson and now I didn't trust anyone easily.

What a senior Bollywood journalist did to me was wrong. I hated her from the bottom of my heart and if this is what competition and insecurity tends to make people do here then I hate this industry just as much.

13

The Hospital Beat

The repercussion of the Akbar Ali fiasco was that now I didn't get to do the big interviews. I only had to cover press conferences or report from hospitals each time a star was admitted—basically stories that were safe and the information readily available to all, so there were less chances of going wrong.

Lilavati Hospital, a multi-speciality hospital in Bandra, a Mumbai suburb, was where I mostly headed to. Most high profile actors chose to come here for treatment.

Sometime in November 2005, I got a tip from another reporter, 'Amitabh Bachchan has been admitted to Lilavati.'

I rushed to my desk, put my mobile charger in my bag, made sure I had enough money in my bag for snacks in case I needed to be there for long. I reached Lilavati Hospital with my cameraman and saw reporters hovering near the gate, all glued to their respective mobile phones. Security had been tightened at the hospital gate to control the media.

As Abhishek Bachchan's black Audi entered the lane, photographers climbed the hospital walls to get a picture. Abhishek got off at the entrance of the hospital door and rushed inside; it took him exactly three seconds to do that and the photographers tried to get the best shot—but not everybody was successful.

'Oh man! Couldn't get a clear shot. That car came in the middle,' said a photographer.

Another one complained, 'I only got his back.'

The photographer of a tabloid groaned, 'Why couldn't he wait for one minute? What was the hurry?'

There was much frenzy in the media present.

One could hear news channel reporters doing live telecast from the gate, 'Just now Abhishek Bachchan has come to the hospital to meet his father. He was alone. He had a yellow bag in his hands, maybe it had home food for Mr Bachchan.'

Now that Jr Bachchan had gone inside, there wouldn't be any action outside the hospital. So we could all take a 10 minute breather. It was Candies time. A popular fast food joint, Candies was in one of the bylanes of Bandra, a two-minute walk from Lilavati. Photographers walked towards the tea stall opposite Lilavati and some reporters headed to Candies—the rest waited in case Bachchan Sr. got any celebrity visitors.

As they chose to stay back, the rest of us could take a break peacefully.

A few hours later good friend of the Bachchans and politician Amar Singh arrived and so did the designated spokesperson, who addressed the media on the actor's condition.

'He is fine but still in the ICU; resting. There is nothing to worry.'

I stuck my head out and yelled, 'Sir, when will we see him back on the big screen?'

Amar Singh snapped at me, 'I can't believe that you are asking such a stupid question. We are worried about his health.'

I could sense that all the reporters were looking and waiting for me to react, and I did, 'But sir that is what his fans would want to know.'

He snapped once again, 'We know that his fans are worried about his health. So I am not going to answer this silly question. If you have any other question you can ask.'

I withdrew here and other journalists took over…

'Sir, did you meet him?'

'Is he talking to the family?'

'How long does he have to stay at the hospital?'

On the same day, good-looking actor John Abraham, who had a major fan following, especially female fans, was also admitted to Lilavati; though the media kept an eye on that too, their main focus was Amitabh Bachchan.

After a couple of days, the news of Amitabh Bachchan's discharge from the hospital reached us, obviously leaked by somebody in the hospital. A few hours later the news of his discharge was confirmed to the media. We were told that he would be discharged the next morning at 10 a.m. so there was ample time to get ready.

The media gathered in front of Lilavati from as early as 7 a.m. Even I was doing live updates for my channel. Photographers, cameramen, reporters, editors and OB Vans had gathered, ready to roll live shots as soon as Mr Bachchan walked out.

It was 10:30 a.m. and there was no sign of the superstar.

An impatient photographer looked at me and asked, 'Hey Raghu! Who gave you guys this information about his discharge?'

I was also not in a very good mood after the long wait. Like him, I too was relying on the news given by the hospital authorities.

I snapped back, 'The hospital! Who else? If you don't want to wait why don't you leave?'

Snubbed, he immediately turned away and started checking his camera.

A few minutes went by and suddenly the photographers started yelling, 'Sir, one look here. Mr Bachchan please look here.'

You could hear non-stop camera clicks. I could barely see anything, as I was not very tall.

Mr Bachchan graciously waited for the media who had been waiting outside the hospital for days. He then left, followed by his fleet of cars. Some enthusiastic reporters followed the cars, thereby causing a jam from Bandra to Juhu.

Now we wouldn't have to report to Lilavati every morning.

'May God always keep Mr Bachchan healthy,' some said aloud as we reporters left the hospital.

Mr Bachchan was back in the hospital on his 66th Birthday in 2008, and so were we! We looked at the familiar faces and laughed. There were also several new faces as reporters would keep quitting and jumping channels. This time his stay was for a few days.

As I covered the hospitals for the Bollywood beat, I was assigned to the Lilavati Hospital several times to report on producer Yash Johar's demise in 2004, Saif Ali Khan's two hospitalisations, to name a few.

We also visited the hospital for good news—when Hrithik Roshan became a father, here at Lilavati or when Kajol and Ajay Devgan had a daughter at Breach Candy Hospital.

By now, I had made friends with the security staff of almost all the popular hospitals. Initially they would push us out of the way. Now they only requested, 'Arre Raghu, please *door se shooting kar yaar. Aage mat aa, hamara boss chilata hai re khali fokat me*. (Arre Raghu, shoot from far. Don't go inside or we will be reprimanded by our boss.)' What used to be an order earlier was now a request.

I didn't have a problem doing stories on this beat but some reporters did not like visiting hospitals. For instance, Ambika who reported for Khabar TV told us that hospitals made her ill; so much so that once when she had fallen really ill, her parents had to force her to get admitted. The first time she was sent out to report she threw up and almost fainted.

Her editor however refused to understand her problem, so now the reporters on the field helped her out.

If she was asked to report from a hospital she called one of us, who she knew would be on duty at the same venue. So she stayed at a distance from the hospital—most of the times at a coffee shop—and we helped her cameraperson with shots and soundbytes. Although the cameramen pulled her leg, calling her a *patient*, most of them were very helpful; they didn't go back and complain that she didn't report from location. Even if she was asked to do a live link on the current situation of a celebrity's health, her cameraman made sure that he set up the camera at a distance from the hospital.

Fortunately the cameramen and even the reporters of the other channels, technically her rivals, understood her problem but her bosses refused to acknowledge it.

14

Oscar Fever and Thereafter

One of the most interesting experiences while writing about Bollywood was reporting on Danny Boyle's *Slumdog Millionaire* that won awards the world over, and that included impressing the jury of the Academy Awards. Though it was an international project, people back home, especially the film fraternity, took pride in it as though it had been made by one of our *desi* directors. I must admit that we media too created a lot of hype around the film, creating headlines each time the film won accolades; at times way over the top.

However, the film also generated a lot of protests. Some people living in slums were upset with Danny Boyle, the director of the film, for calling them Slum *Dogs*.

Danny and his team were in India to interact with the media before the film was released. At the press conference I got the opportunity to ask the first question.

'Hi Danny, this is Raghu from News 24x7, a lot of people living in the slums are upset with the word *slumdog* in the title. There have been some protests in Mumbai over this. What would you like to tell them?'

Danny apologised, 'I didn't mean to hurt anyone, but if I did, I regret it deeply and would like to take this opportunity to apologise.'

This public apology from the filmmaker managed to assuage a lot of anger. I knew that Amitabh Bachchan and Shah Rukh Khan had turned down the role that finally went to Anil Kapoor. I had another question for Boyle. I raised my hand.

The organiser was irritated with me, 'One last question Raghu.'

Since this was the filmmaker's first press conference in India there was quite a formidable media turnout.

'Sir, which Bollywood actor will you cast in your next film, Amitabh Bachchan or Shah Rukh Khan?'

He laughed and said that he would love to work with both someday, adding that he would also love to work with Aamir Khan. That had his audience laughing and clapping. After Danny, most of the questions were for Dev and Freida. She was very articulate and smart whereas Dev appeared mischievous; he even imitated Anil Kapoor.

Our job now was to find the child actors in the film. Word had spread that Rubina and Azhar stayed in Dharavi.

My news editor ordered, 'Raghu dig out the kids; they live in Dharavi.'

Now that is quite a vague direction for someone who would now have to walk through the maze of Asia's largest slum. I was unsuccessful and my editor was wrong. Another channel found the kids in Bairampada which is another slum in Bandra East.

I finally managed to find the place after enquiring with some other reporters who had visited the place. It was mucky, smelly and highly populated, with kids playing around in the dirt. There was a dirty drain flowing in front of the long line of houses. I wondered at the bravery of the team that had researched for the film to create the perfect look; navigating through these lanes was something that even we Mumbaikars would dread.

Rubina's father, high on alcohol, was not too happy to see me, asking me point-blank how this interview would benefit the family. After a lot of requests he agreed to a five minute interview with Rubina. She was a very sweet girl, clueless about why we were interested in talking to her. It was so ironical that a film that had left the filmgoers awestruck had failed to really touch the lives of some who were so integral to making it a success.

The day the Golden Globes were announced we had a line up of guests, related to the film, at our studio. The co-director of the film, Loveleen Tandan, left no stone unturned to promote the film in India; she was seen in practically all news channels.

On the day of the Oscars we reached office at 4 a.m. IST to watch the awards ceremony live. We were ready to report on it as soon as the bulletins started at 6 a.m. Entertainment and city reporters were sent out to speak to those in Bollywood who were associated with the film; some went to interview Gulzar who didn't go for the Oscars because of a shoulder injury.

I found myself outside Sukhvinder Singh's house to get his reaction. He had sung the popular song 'Jai Ho' but had not been invited by the producers to attend the Oscars.

He saw Rahman singing and told the waiting media, 'I wish they had taken me to sing "Jai Ho."'

This was big news.

Singer of 'Jai Ho' upset was the flash for the channels.

We now waited for the members of the cast to return to India. Resul Pookutty, Irrfan Khan and the kids were to return to Mumbai two days after the ceremony and Rahman was to fly straight to Chennai. I was at the Chhatrapati Shivaji Terminus, Mumbai, waiting for their arrival. The same night Kylie Minogue had also landed in India to shoot for a film with Akshay Kumar.

All the print and TV reporters and photographers were at the airport having cutting *chai* at regular intervals to try and stay awake and be alert for the stars to arrive. A big crowd was also waiting at the airport to welcome them, inspite of the late hour. Finally, at around 2 a.m. Resul and Irrfan Khan walked out. The actors posed for the cameras and gave sound bytes.

The crowd of spectators and media soon got out of control and the actors had to be whisked out in a police van to avoid the crowd. We later learnt that they got into their own cars on the highway.

Next morning, we were back at the airport, this time to welcome Rubina and Azhar. After getting their shots and sound bytes, the news channel reporters followed them home. Rubina's father got angry seeing the media and started pushing the cameramen.

Because of the international recognition, the kids from *Slumdog Millionaire* were invited for the Filmfare Awards, the biggest Film Awards ceremony in India. The enthusiastic kids from Behrampada slums reached the venue (Yashraj Studios) at 6:30 p.m, while it's common knowledge that no film awards ceremony kicked off before 9 p.m. The kids had no choice but to wait outside the gate for the person who was carrying their passes.

And that's when the problem started.

Some Hindi channels reported that the kids who were back from the Oscars had been insulted and made to wait for hours outside the venue of an award function. Those who had invited them should have informed them that the award ceremony would start post 9:30 p.m.

Rubina and Azhar finally got to step inside after 9:30 p.m. and their anger was assuaged as they were invited on stage by none other than Shah Rukh Khan. Even as we watched the euphoria all around, at this international recognition, Abdul Bhai, a senior cameraman from Khabar TV, suddenly asked me, 'Do you think it was a good idea to create all this hype around Rubina and Azhar?

'I mean today they have seen so much—Oscars, Filmfare, filmstars, glamour and even America—and now they have to go back to the slums they live in. Once this frenzy around them dies down, they won't get all this importance. How will it feel then?'

He had a good point.

I responded, 'Abdul Bhai, there are two options in their life, according to me. Either they get to see all this for a short period of time, or they continue to live their usual life never experiencing something like this ever. You decide, which one is a greater loss?'

A veteran cameraman, Abdul Bhai was aware of the flitting nature of fame, 'Remember what I said… Fame is a bad thing. After a few years, when they are all by themselves, unacknowledged by the very people who showered them with praises, they will find it very difficult.'

'I understand what you are saying Abdul Bhai and somewhere I agree with you but like I said, it's how you look at the bigger picture,' I retorted.

Somewhere inside I totally agreed with him but I wouldn't have stated the obvious. I knew both Rubina and Azhar would be forgotten with time and they would get back to the tough life they came from. One thing I was totally convinced about was, '*Fame is a bad thing*.'

15

Luck by Chance

After the Akbar Ali incident, I was lying low, but continued working hard to regain the trust of my bosses. Covering events, press conferences, hospital visits, I could make out that I was looked upon as *the reporter who made a mistake* in our bureau.

It had been two years with News 24x7 and those who joined with me were either Principal Correspondents or Special Correspondents.

My designation hadn't changed till now. I was still a Correspondent.

I hadn't even got a raise like everyone else. I was told that since the company was spending on a legal fight with actor Akbar Ali, because of me, I would not be getting any increment till that was resolved. One incident had stopped my growth! I was not assigned important shoots so I did not get the opportunity to do good interviews; all that I got to cover were little tidbits of news regarding the industry that were sometimes used and sometimes just discarded.

But things changed, and rather drastically, albeit not under very happy circumstances.

One day, when I was on my way home on my bike and crossing Mahim station, I heard loud blasts; two loud ones, back to back. The ear-splitting blast caused immediate commotion around me; everyone started running.

I stopped my bike and looked towards the tracks. A portion of one train had been ripped apart. There was a lot of smoke. People were screaming. My first reaction was to call the police control room. Then I immediately called Kamble, now the Managing Editor of the channel.

'Sir…sir…there has been a bomb blast at Mahim station, inside the train. The compartment has been ripped apart.'

Kamble was understandably shocked, 'What? When? Are you sure? How do you know?'

'Sir, I am right here! There is a lot of commotion. I will shoot with my phone and send you some images. I have a 3G connection and will try and send you a 10-second clip right away. Send me a camera unit.'

I could hear Kamble shouting in the newsroom before I disconnected my call, 'All units, reporters…to the Mahim station. Get there fast! Bomb blasts in the city. Desk team, call 100 and check what information they have. Put Raghu on air. He is right there! This is breaking news and I don't want any delay or mistakes.'

I tried to gather as much information as possible but it was too early to get any official estimate. All I got to know was that the power grid for the area had been shut down to prevent further damage. Hence, all the trains had come to standstill. By the time I sent one photo I got a call from a Delhi number for a live phoner. I heard the anchor saying, 'We are getting some *breaking news* from Mumbai. There have been two blasts at Mahim station and our reporter Raghu Kumar is right there. Over to you Raghu.'

I immediately responded, 'I am right here at the Mahim station. Two compartments of a local train have been ripped apart by the blasts. All trains have been stopped due to the power failure. Cops are now vacating the area, asking people to leave the station. I can see a lot of fire engines rushing to the spot.'

'Raghu, how many people have been injured in this blast?' The anchor asked.

I moved closer to the disaster spot to give a clearer picture, 'It's peak hour and the train compartments in the Western line are usually full at this hour. (I walked close to the compartment and saw injured people and bodies literally falling down from the train. The scene was quite horrific with blood and painful cries everywhere.) I can see some dead bodies but will be able to confirm the number of dead only when the official figures are out.'

The anchor asked, 'Raghu, what else do you see around you? Tell us.'

'Some of the compartments are on fire so the fire engines are trying to put that off first. Fire fighters are trying to get people out of the compartment at the earliest. The police are trying to keep bystanders away, to avoid more casualties of fire, but locals are helping the injured and carrying them to the ambulances.'

The anchor discontinued the live feed, saying, 'Okay, Raghu stay with us. We have the Commissioner of Mumbai on the phone with us…'

I hung up to take photos from my phone. They would call me back.

Till the anchor talked to the commissioner, on air, I took about seven to eight photos and a 10-second clip of the blast site and sent it to the input desk, in the office, marking everyone I could think of.

And that was it! Suddenly, no one could make calls anymore; cell phones were jammed across the city.

I could not see any other reporter in sight for the next 10 minutes. Half an hour later, other channels like News India, Planet News, 24 Khabrein reached the spot. The reporters could not communicate with their respective channels because the phones were down. I was happy that I could break the news with my channel, which now had some photos and a small clip to run.

Soon I spotted Andy; he had come alone. He saw me and told me to take the microphone and start talking to people. I took first hand account of those who had helped the injured.

Andy continued to shoot and I rushed to the office on my bike, with the tape. There was a crazy jam on the roads, especially those leading to the Mahim station. I took the narrow bylanes and made it to the office in 20 minutes. The interviews that I took and shots that Andy took were played again; these were the first proper visuals to be played on any channel.

The Commissioner of Mumbai said on air that he heard about the blasts through News 24x7.

The whole night went off in a flurry of activities—injesting tapes (process of transferring content of *tape* to compressed digital hard disk storage), reporting live, and going to the hospitals to get the details. I got to go home only the next morning.

When I was back at work, I learnt that a mail had come from Kranti, addressing the entire bureau. There was a special mention of me since I was the first to report and even send photos from my camera. He was all praises for me, particularly complimenting me on my presence of mind.

Kamble called me to his office. Now his cabin was much bigger than before. 'You are back! Great job young man.

You were at the right place at the right time,' he said as he hugged me.

I realised the irony of the situation and did not hesitate to put it into words, 'Thanks sir! It's sad that we call a bomb blast site the *right place* and such an unfortunate incident brings me glory. But thanks anyway.'

Kamble understood. 'We are in the news business. Blasts are bad news but you did a good job of reporting it.'

Rajeev called to tell me how his channel, especially the big bosses, went crazy when all they could see was News 24x7 with latest visuals and my voice reporting from Mahim station.

The next day, the news channels had a lot more clarity on what happened and a lot of official announcements were made.

I turned up the volume on my final report on this story, 'The bombs were placed in two pressure cookers; one went off in the first class compartment and the other in the second class. Many were injured and 187 people died.' *(http://www.dnaindia.com/mumbai/report-mumbai-2006-train-bomb-blast-accused-studies-in-jail-1916765)*

So many dead. I felt terrible as I watched the visuals of the ripped train compartments. Though I was happy that I reported on this first and my channel was being praised because of me, I couldn't be elated because of the nature of the news. It took two years and an incident like a blast that killed 209 people—for me to prove my worth in my news channel and bounce back to mainstream reporting.

During that time, my mom said something that always stayed with me, 'Good things happen to good people.' It could have been any other reporter there, but it was me. I hate to call a *bomb blast site* the *right place*... It's far from it.

16

Rising Star

Now that I was back in business, I felt a lot more confident. My bosses were giving me opportunities to report on big stories. I could sense the difference in the way people conducted themselves with me. There was respect; thanks to the coverage of the blasts. My bosses had realised that I was good in *Breaking News* situations and I was one of the first ones to be sent out when such a situation arose.

When it came to the Bollywood beat, I was now sent to interview the big stars. This helped me earn more points as stars like Aamir Khan, for instance, rarely spoke to news channels. I was also the chosen one when it came to reporting on the film awards; for the IIFA awards, I travelled to different countries.

I had made friends with a lot of PR people; they now called me to check if a particular day was good for a press conference. I had become the *go-to person* for the PR fraternity. Since we had a daily show and needed a lot of content, I helped them plug their stories on our shows. It was a mutually beneficial relationship; their events helped to fill our daily show and their clients were happy because their events got coverage in reputed news channels.

In the next six months I achieved as much as a reporter could in the TV medium. I was on TV every night—at times interviewing top stars or sometimes just hosting the show. Producers would call me every Friday to update me with the box-office collections of their latest releases, ensuring I write good things about their business. I knew most of the figures they gave me were rubbish and fudged!

If stars didn't turn up, I boycotted the event. Then it was boycotted by the entire media. This was a practice with the reporters in Bollywood; primarily done to teach the actors a lesson so that they respected our time and came on time. A lot of times my friends in the PR business would joke, 'My actor is coming late, don't start your boycott*giri* here please.'

My problem was not just with actors coming in late at an event, but with their non-apologetic attitude. It was this that made their behaviour into a habit. Since I had established good relations with the top actors, they too preferred approaching me when they wanted to communicate with their audience before a film release or if they were planning something big.

To my delight, News 24x7 decided to give me a film review segment, *Raghu's Report*. This was the segment a lot of producers feared. I tried to emulate Rajeev since his show was hugely popular. I was not just invited for regular press shows but film previews were organised where I would be specially invited.

It had become an usual practice for film PRO's to call me on a Monday morning to ask, 'Raghu sir, when and where would you like to watch our movie?' I often had requests from my reporter colleagues, who wanted to come and watch a film when it was previewed for me. I never said '*No*' to them, particularly to the junior reporters. I knew how hard they were struggling to make a name for themselves; I had been in their place not too long ago.

During Diwali and other festivals, fancy gifts were sent home by producers and actors. My mom and sister revelled at my success as a Bollywood reporter.

As the financial year drew to a close I was in for a big surprise.

Seeing my work and growing popularity, the company gifted me a car and shares in News 24x7.

The keys to my new car were handed over to me by the CEO, Rama Raghvan. 'Congratulations Raghu, you deserve it. Next year, same time, it should be an SUV for you.'

I was on cloud nine!

It was a vindication of sorts to receive accolades from the company that had written me off. Also, this climb on the success charts was happening in front of Shereen, who was keeping a really low profile after her break-up with Alok Mittal's nephew. She had fallen out of favour with the Mittals and wasn't invited to any of their private parties.

I opened a twitter account and soon filmstars were following me. Not surprisingly, I also had lakhs of other followers as well, who I guess were film buffs. Actors retweeted my thoughts and views on a regular basis. It wasn't long before I reached the 25 lakh followers mark. It was an achievement as no entertainment journalist has ever reached that mark.

This was a period of several highs for me…

The most popular FM station in India, 101 FM, decided to tie up with News 24x7 to have an audio version of *Raghu's Reviews*. The result was that people were not just watching me on their television sets but were listening to me as they drove around in their cars. The icing on the cake was when I was nominated in the Best Entertainment Anchor category of the year's most popular TV awards.

I won three out of the four awards.

I decided to boycott the academy that didn't give me the Best Anchor trophy. 'Why should I attend their function if they don't think I am good enough to win the Best Anchor Award. Screw them,' I told my colleagues, family and friends when they asked me.

Nobody pointed it out then, but ego was destroying my personality, slowly and gradually. The confidence that I could do my job well had now turned into vanity. Finally, the only problem that had troubled me was also solved. Akbar Ali called me over for dinner and settled everything across the table.

'Raghu, you and I are from the media industry. It would be best if we are friends rather than enemies,' he said warmly.

We shook hands over this and he told his lawyers to withdraw the case against me and News 24x7. I immediately did an extensive interview with Akbar Ali, which was played on high rotation (repeated reruns) since he didn't do too many interviews.

It didn't take long for word to spread that Akbar and I were now friends. It was one big load off my back.

My reporter friends asked me for a treat and we found ourselves in a nightclub in Bandra. I was game for a celebration. The case was over! But how had this come about. Obviously, my growing popularity as a reporter had got Akbar Ali to do some introspection.

17

On Cloud Nine

Success at work and popularity together brought in a certain swaggering confidence in my personality. From somebody who was accepting what was being doled out, I now began to demand certain privileges. Reena was quick to point this out as an *attitudinal shift*, whereas my mom just chided me for having become more short-tempered.

As for my professional life, I always took only my favourite cameraman Andy for my shoots. A couple of times I had insisted that he come for a shoot even on the days when he was off. I had not hesitated to show my anger when an alternative was offered. Andy had always fallen in with my plans and I never found out whether this heckled him. A couple of times I had even cancelled my shoots because Andy was not available and now the production bosses ensured that Andy was available whenever I needed him.

I had other perks as well; I could now do the edits with my favourite editor, Sameer, and even go for the shoots in the cars of my choice.

I got away with all this…and was confident that I would be able to.

When one is riding high, the channel is willing to pamper, more so as it work for them too.

The market was abuzz with the news of an upcoming channel backed by the country's top business family, the Singhanias. I knew them quite well because their younger son, Yash Singhania, was a film producer.

Yash called me over for dinner one day and told me that his father, Raj Kumar Singhania, wanted to meet me. I accepted the invitation for dinner at their sea-facing bungalow in South Mumbai.

After a good dinner and some laughs over Yash's flop movies, which I had ripped apart on my show, *Raghu Reviews*, the Singhania patriarch asked me to accompany him to his office on the top floor. Yash informed me that he had to make a couple of calls.

So it was just Raj Kumar Singhania and me in his plush office, whose windows offered a breathtaking view of the Arabian Sea. The uniformed attendant shut the door behind us. I could gauge what this meeting was all about.

Singhania senior, known to be an astute businessman came right to the point. 'Raghu, you are a nice guy. I like you. I am investing Rs 300 crores in an entertainment channel. I want you to head the editorial. You can build up your team, appoint people you want to work with. Give this venture a good direction. Take your time but make it the number one lifestyle and entertainment channel in three years. Don't worry about your contract for this job. We will work that out the way you want because if you are happy I am happy.'

At the age of 28, it was too good an offer to refuse. But I still asked for a few days to think about it.

'Take a week or two. Come back and let's get started. I don't believe in wasting time,' Singhania's firm handshake was a 100 per cent confirmation from his side.

I went back home and discussed it with my sister and mom. But my family never interfered with my professional decisions. I spoke to Rajeev who helped me weigh the pros and cons of the offer; I would be giving up my well-established position for a start-up. But then the Singhanias meant big money and the opportunity to call the shots completely. At this stage in my career, I could afford to take the risk.

Within a week I took up the offer. I requested the Singhanias not to make this public till I had informed News 24x7.

Same day, I wrote to the Mittals. I only told them that I wanted to move on; I didn't mention anything about the offer.

The first reaction was Kamble calling me to his cabin.

'Tell me one thing. Have you taken a decision or are you willing to negotiate?'

'I think I have taken a decision,' I said confidently, sipping on my coffee.

'Okay Raghu, as long as you know what you are doing with the brand that you have made for yourself I am happy for you and I wish you good luck.'

The bureau head also approached me, speaking to me on behalf of Alok Mittal who was travelling. I declined the offer and put in my papers.

The next day I had an unexpected caller. It was Rani Mittal, Alok Mittal's wife, 'Raghu what happened? I heard you are leaving us?'

'Yes, ma'am. Have been here for long, I guess. Want to try out new things,' I responded, masking my surprise. I had never spoken to her earlier.

'Can we talk about it? You are like a son! Don't take any hasty decision. If there is anything that is not working for you here, please don't hesitate to tell me.'

'No ma'am, it's not a hasty decision. I have thought about it. Although I must say it is thanks to News 24x7 that I am what I am today.'

'So would you not like to come and meet Alok before you make a final decision to leave?'

'I will have some time on hand once I quit so I will surely drop by,' I said, making it clear that I was not likely to change my decision.

She understood. 'Good luck Raghu.'

'Thanks ma'am.'

Soon after I had hung up, Rajeev texted me, asking me to meet him for dinner. But I had to refuse as I was scheduled to meet Akbar Ali. I promised to meet him in a day or two.

I knew that Rajeev wanted to talk to me about Singhania's offer. But I really didn't need advice now. Why would I? Haven't I made it on my own so far?

Andy was upset too but it was difficult for me to meet everybody and explain my decision. So I just cancelled all dinner and coffee plans and focussed only on moving ahead.

The news about my quitting News 24x7 also made it to the newspapers since I hosted a popular show. *News 24x7 loses its lead player* said most of the newspapers.

The company hired a young man, Mihir, to replace me. He was a confident guy but I personally didn't think he had what I had.

I did not hesitate to let this be known to my reporter friends, adding, 'Do they really think they can get a novice to replace me? That is not going to work.'

To my surprise Mihir called me one day, asking for advice.

I had no patience with him and did not care to give any advice. In fact, I was quite vocal about it, 'Dude, I wish you luck but don't call me again. No one gave me any advice when I started working. Make your own rules and win your own battles the way I did.'

And I hung up.

I started the pre-launch work and it took us six months of back-breaking work to get things in order. In those six months I had spent days and nights in the office getting things sorted—from the look of our studios, to getting the logo designed to getting the interiors of our new office ready.

I didn't socialise at all during this period; I didn't even meet Rajeev or Andy. I just worked the whole day and went back home to sleep.

After six to eight months, our channel Glitterati was ready to go on air. A big launch party was planned where the logo would be unveiled and the who's who of the industry would be present. I received bouquets from actors at my swanky office in South Mumbai.

The PR agency engaged by the channel lined up some interviews for me; from taking interviews, now I was busy giving *gyaan* to business reporters.

The party was attended by not just actors but also politicians known to the Singhanias. My family was present too and my sister was more than happy to see her favourite actors. My mom was very happy to see my success.

Rajeev too dropped by briefly to wish me luck. He had been sent an invite by our event management company. I know I should have called him myself but it just slipped my mind. But Rajeev didn't have qualms about such things; he walked in with a big bouquet, 'Big man! You don't have time to meet. Best of luck. This is huge. Handle it well.'

I hugged him and asked him to join Glitterati.

'Nah! I am happy where I am right now,' he declined my offer with a warm smile and again wished me luck before leaving.

I had never thought that one day I would offer Rajeev Mehra a job.

The channel went on air. My show was a celebrity chat show, shot in the studios, called *One on One with Raghu Kumar*. We started canning shows with the top stars and recorded five episodes every week.

My responsibilities did not include taking care of the daily content; an input desk and an output desk took care of that along with the reporters. I was more involved with the big meeting where we discussed TRPs, the reach of the channel, competition and marketing.

Glitterati had hired many interns from the best journalism colleges of India. Most of these incumbents were in complete awe of me and I must say I enjoyed it when they came to take pictures with me or looked at me with wonder in their eyes.

Soon after our launch I was invited by the best journalism colleges to give guest lectures. I declined unless they involved a good monetary gain. I asked my secretary to tactfully avoid the unwanted invitations, saying that I was travelling extensively.

If I had to go to an important place or attend an important function, Singhania Senior would inform me. Frankly, I quite enjoyed wining and dining with the crème de la crème of the Mumbai high society.

I was very happy with the way my career had panned out. I had everything that I could aspire for and I often told myself that life was simply beautiful.

18

Getting Back

One morning when I was on my way to work I got a call from an unknown number. I never answered calls if I didn't recognise the number; I knew that if people wanted to get in touch with me they would either send a text message or find their way to reach me.

The calls, from the same number, continued for some time and then stopped just as suddenly.

I had come a long way from the time I used to travel by local buses to the office.

Now I travelled comfortably in the car and used my travel time—rather a long one, from Chembur to South Mumbai—to read newspapers in the car. I preferred the main newspapers, which had real news, to the tabloids which were full of sycophant stories on actors; I knew that the actors paid the newspapers to publish whatever they wanted.

Soon my phone beeped, and I picked it up to read the message. It read, '*Hi Raghu. This is Vijay Kapoor. Your childhood friend. Amit Kapoor's son. Do you remember me? Do call when you get this message. Have been trying to reach you. Waiting eagerly for your call.*'

I knew Vijay had become an actor like his dad but was not a patch on his dad's talent and not half as popular as him. Vijay's debut film had bombed and his career was going nowhere after he gave a dozen flops in a row. He was one of those actors who you would see in multi-starrers, doing two-bit roles of the second lead or other insignificant roles. I wondered why he was calling me after so many years and that too after ending our friendship the way he did.

But didn't I know the answer to that?

It was because I was a successful film journalist. Period. If I wasn't, I doubt he would have even bothered finding my number.

He messaged again after a few hours, '*Come on Raghu! You were the one with a bigger heart. Forgive me if you are angry. We were kids dude. Give me a chance to make up for my mistakes!*'

He clearly thought he knew me well. But I was not the same vulnerable kid anymore. I wanted him to realise what it felt like to be ignored.

I called my sister, 'Hello Reena! Guess who has been trying to get in touch with me?'

'Amitabh Bachchan?' She responded, sounding excited.

'No! Are you mad?'

'Katrina Kaif?' She said, sounding a bit disappointed.

'No! Can you only think of celebrities? In a way, this fellow is also a celebrity. I meant, Vijay Kapoor.'

She laughed out loudly and then remarked in a mocking tone, 'That loser! He has come back to you. What did he say?'

'He has sent me two texts.'

Reena yelled out to mom, 'Mom, Vijay Kapoor wants to be part of Raghu's life again. Returned like a bad penny.'

Mom asked with her usual sweetness, 'How is he?'

Reena snapped, 'We don't know and we don't care.'

She came back on the phone, 'This feels great Raghu. People who insulted you and walked out of your life now want to come back. Just ask him to get lost.'

'You are so predictable Reena; I knew this is how you would react. *Chalo* I'm hanging up.'

I kept thinking about it. Reena was right. I shouldn't let him back into my life. How could I forget how easily he had walked out of my life and made new friends, while I was left alone? Of course, the friends I made then, who were not as rich as him, are still my friends. How can I forgive his father for making us realise that we were not rich or that we were suffering because we didn't have a father. I could forgive Vijay because he had been too young then and was influenced by his father, but why did he not get in touch with me when I was in college? Why not before he made his Bolywood debut? Why didn't he bother calling me for the much hyped premiere of his first film? I didn't have an answer to all this and frankly I didn't care.

I didn't want to get back to Vijay. I wanted him to go through the same helpless feeling which I had experienced when he had walked out of my life, wanted him to understand what it was like being deliberately ignored.

My mom did tell me a couple of times to forgive and forget. 'If you do the same thing then you are no different.'

'But he did it first, mom.'

I must admit it felt nice to know that I was important enough for them to grovel. Maybe sadistic, but what the hell! It was a great feeling.

But then, since mom insisted, I decided to give him a chance. Mom said, 'Arrogance is not a good thing.'

I replied and asked him to meet me at a coffee shop in Bandra. He immeditely replied and we fixed a time to catch up.

I reached on time and he was nowhere to be seen. I waited for 15 minutes and sent him a text saying I have to leave for some work. He called back, 'I am so sorry, dude! I'm reaching in five!'

I ordered some coffee and waited for the hero to come. He came after 10 minutes. I got up to shake hands, he came forward to hug me, I obliged. I was not very happy about waiting for almost 30 minutes but he didn't seem to be very apologetic about it. I guess Bollywood had spoilt him enough.

Vijay was loud and flamboyant. He was wearing a silver jacket and had shades on his head though it was evening. It felt awkward to start the conversation because I really didn't have anything to say.

'*Tu* reporter *kaise ban gaya be?* (How the hell did you become a reporter?)' he laughed.

I sensed some sarcasm but I just smiled.

'*Yaar tu hamare group mein sabse* useless *hua karta tha! Aur aaj dekh, tu kuch ban gaya.* (You were the most uselss boy in our group! And today, you have made it big in life.) Not bad Raghu Kumar!'

'As far as I remember, our group had just two people, you and me. You were the son of a superstar and you are still struggling and I didn't have any great family backing and I did make it by myself. So you should be proud of me.'

'Hey! For your kind information I have done 20 films. What do you mean by I'm struggling?'

'Yes! Out of which 18 have flopped Vijay and two were multi-starrers so you shouldn't take credit for those, so it's time you put your ego aside and talk to me like a friend.'

'Balls! My 18 films have flopped according to you?'

'Vijay, we are at a crowded coffee shop in Bandra and no one recognises you here! But if you look around it does look like they recognise me very well. Even the staff here knows my name.'

'You come on TV *yaar*. I come in films. My one film releases in six months; it takes that much time to shoot. Journalists bark on TV all day so they obviously end up seeing the shit on TV.'

'Aamir Khan does one film a year but people recognise him *na*. So shut your trap. I thought you called me to make up! You are a sick, pathetic brat and I regret meeting you.' I pushed the table and got up. People around were looking at us because we both were quite loud.

'Dude! Sorry! Why are you getting angry?'

'Because you should be apologising for how you behaved with me when we were kids.' I was angry. I continuted, 'You have no respect for me and nor for my work clearly. You think journalists bark right?'

'Sorry, I was angry. I didn't mean it,' Vijay was on back foot.

'Why did you want to meet me?' I asked.

'I'll be frank. You must be knowing Karan Johar *na*. *Mujhe* please *ek baar mila de*,' he requested. 'Please help me meet Karan Johar.'

'Oh! So you want me to help you. That's all you wanted from me after all these years.'

'No, no! I wanted to meet you. I missed you *yaar*.'

'You are sick Vijay! Even now you just think of yourself. You only know how to use people. First go and learn some manners. Get out of my face and never call me again.' I stormed out of the coffee shop. I could hear him grumbling behind my back but I didn't bother.

It did hurt because I was expecting something nice out of this meeting. I never told mom or Reena that I met this idiot. Mom would feel bad and Reena would get more angry. I always knew that's how these *filmi* types are. I thought my childhood friend would have changed since he messaged me but I was wrong. I was happy this time I walked out on him.

19

Ups and Downs

I was not a simple *boy next door* anymore. I was a new person—successful, confident and self made. I had learnt that one had to be shrewd to be successful in this business. In fact, that was one quality I saw working for most people in the media industry. A simple and ordinary person would never survive here… Therefore, these were the traits I quickly abandoned.

I didn't have too many friends because most of my time was spent working. However, it was work when I chanced upon Apeksha. She was the host of a travel channel, who I had come across during an event at Taj Lands End. She was pretty, light eyed with straight brown hair. I liked her friendly and down-to-earth nature. The first time we met at the Taj was for a travel portal's press conference. I was there because a film actor was supposed to launch their new product. I was used to filmstars so waiting for them was no big deal. Apeksha sat right next to me at the press conference and she seemed irriated about it. 'Why can't film actors come on time?' she asked me.

I smiled, 'They are never on time and that's how Bollywood is.'

'Oh yes! You must be used to their tantrums. But come on, aren't they paid for this? So shouldn't they be professional about it?'

'Well! They are paid for almost everything. They are paid to do a film but they never reach the sets on time. That's how they are, unprofessional! I have come to terms with it.'

'Is there any actor who comes on time?'

'Yes! Amitabh Bachchan does. He is always on time!'

'Wow! No wonder he is Amitabh Bachchan!'

We bumped into each other at various such events and soon we started texting and catching up over coffee. I liked the idea that I could have a decent conversation with her. The innocuous chats over cups of coffee became romantic dates and soon she was at my place to meet mom and Reena. They took to her immediately. In spite of the fact that she was very successful and travelled to the best places in the world, she had no airs about her.

After a six-month courtship, we decided to get married. Our respective families were very happy and December 2, 2010, was fixed as the wedding day.

My wedding ceremony was private, just for family members, but the reception was loud. The venue was the Mumbai Turf Club. The VIP entrance led the celebrities straight up to the stage. Every single star I had got acquainted with attended the wedding reception.

Most of my cousins kept coming to me while I was on stage asking me to introduce them to the stars.

Apeksha too was conscious of the star presence around us. At one point she murmured, 'I am feeling really awkward with all these celebrities here. Hope I am looking good.'

'You are looking gorgeous,' I assured her and added, 'Like a star yourself.'

Mr Singhania too walked up to us and congratulated me. 'You are lucky Raghu to find such a pretty girl and that too somebody who works in the media. An ideal match! Hope you have a good time in Switzerland. God bless.'

'Thank you, sir.' Mr Singhania had gifted me a week-long honeymoon package in Switzerland. Our wedding photos also made it to the party pages of the newspapers since all the stars attended the reception. My cousins were happy because they got to see all the popular film actors they had always wanted to see. Most of these stars made a quick appearance, but my extended family managed to take pictures with almost all of them.

Apeksha and I were soon off on our week-long honeymoon to Switzerland. She was to travel to her Spain office afterwards to report on how the recent economic crisis was affecting tourism and I was to return to Mumbai.

During our trip I got at least 20 calls a day from office; different departments called with their problems and I was busy solving most of it from there, sometimes on the phone and sometimes sending long emails.

'You should learn to detach yourself from work when you travel, else you will never enjoy a holiday,' Apeksha suggested quietly.

I was just glad that she hadn't thrown a big tantrum over this.

'That's true. I have to learn this from you. The channel is still new, so still facing teething problems. We cannot afford to screw up things at this stage because the competition is crazy,' I said in my defence.

The week passed by way too soon and Apeksha was off to Spain while I headed back to Mumbai.

Reena and mom were excited because I had picked up gifts for them. We sat to chat after dinner and I told them about the beauty of Switzerland, promising them that we would plan a family holiday soon.

Once I got back to work I got sucked into the daily grind of meetings and other work related to the channel. This left me with no time for family and friends. After marriage one is expected to attend quite a few dinners and lunches, but in my case, all of that was just waived off. Mom didn't accept any invitation on our behalf because she knew that I hated the traditional lunch and dinner get-togethers. I found them really pretentious and boring; I would rather catch up with friends and relatives informally on weekends.

Apeksha loved animals and as soon as she was back from Spain we decided to get a pet dog; we adopted a six month-old Dachshund. Mom and my sister were also delighted. We named him Pepper and in no time he had become the apple of our eyes. When all of us were together at home, then all our focus was on Pepper.

Meanwhile, work continued to be stressful.

Soon after I re-joined the office, I felt the need to call a meeting with the marketing department to check on the status of all the campaigns that we had planned before I left.

I was take aback completely by the response I got.

I was told by the marketing manager that Raj Kumar Singhania's adopted son Akhil would now be handling all matters related to marketing.

I had single-handedly taken care of all aspects of the channel till a week ago. What had changed suddenly? I decided to take up the matter with Yash directly. I walked into his cabin and asked him directly why I had not been consulted before roping in Akhil.

Yash did not raise his voice but I sensed a hard edge in the way he spoke to me, 'Raghu, remember one thing. The company belongs to us; you work here. Akhil is my step brother so he is also one of the owners of Glitterati. Let's not have this discussion again. Dad wanted Akhil to join, so this matter is above discussion.'

I left the cabin without saying another word, but this incident had made me insecure about my position with Glitterati. I wondered if the channel would be run like a family business. What if some other cousins or step children took over some day?

These questions played on in my mind as I went about my work. I tried to bring in the same kind of enthusiasm to the job, but somewhere my faith in the Singhanias had been shaken.

The work load continued to increase, with erratic working hours and sleepless nights and before I knew it, I had collapsed in the office one day.

My family was informed as I was rushed to the Breach Candy Hospital. Apeksha was about to leave for Dubai for some work but she cancelled her trip. When I regained consciousness in the hospital ICU, I found her sitting next to me.

Seeing me open my eyes, she hugged me and broke down, 'I told you even on our honeymoon that you have taken too much upon yourself. Now no phone calls or emails for a month. Health comes before all the fame and money you want to acquire. Let us take care of that first please.'

Check-ups and tests confirmed that it was a minor heart attack and the doctors advised me to take it easy and stay away from work for at least a month. I was literally under house arrest. I knew for a fact that this time I was not going to have my way out.

I rested; walked in our garden and played with our dog. I watched Glitterati. A ticker scroll said, '*This week the telecast of* One on One with Raghu Kumar *is replaced by India's costly homes*.'

Obviously, we would record some new shows when I got back to work. What I didn't know was that this would never happen.

A lot of food lovingly made by mom, the attention and affection of my new wife and the care given by my sister got me back on my feet in two weeks.

The tests told us that everything was normal; in fact the doctors suggested that I get back to work—all that I had to do was to take things easy.

I called to inform Yash that I would be joining the next day.

'Are you sure? Are you okay? Don't worry about work. We have everything in control.'

'No, no, I am fine, so will see you tomorrow.'

The watchman and the receptionist were delighted to have me back; that's what their beaming smiles told me.

I was told that Raj Kumar Singhania had come to the office and was sitting in Yash's cabin, so the latter had taken my cabin for the day.

Yash got to his feet as I walked in, 'Welcome! Great to have you back! Come let's go to my cabin. Dad wanted to see you.'

We took the elevator to the floor above us, to Yash's office.

Singhania Senior gave me a hug and after checking about my health said, 'Raghu, while you were away we realised that *aaj kal life ka koi bharosa nahi hai* (there are no guarantees in life). We can't have one person doing everything; we must distribute work and that will also be good for you—some rest and some work. I have seen a lot more than you young people have. I know that you youngsters do not believe in taking rest.'

'Sir, I just got back from two weeks of rest,' I smiled.

'Oh shut up! That was forced rest.'

He continued, 'To cut a long story short, Yash is taking over marketing from Akhil, who will join editorial department and share space with you. He is a good-looking, young boy like you and can also do celebrity interviews. It would be good to have a good journalist in the family. Now that we own a channel, what can be a better platform? He is my son, like Yash. Since you are the Managing Editor, I will make him the Editor. I want him to do this, it's my dream. I want you to help him.'

'Sir, but what about me?' I asked, suddenly nervous about my future.

'What about you? You are very much there Raghu? I am just getting my son in.'

'I head the channel and now someone, who knows less than me, is my boss now. It looks terrible on my profile.'

'Raghu, in this channel business I know much less than you do, but does that mean I am not your boss?'

I argued, my agitation now apparent in my voice, 'Sir, you have earned it. And so have I.'

'Raghu! You are crossing your limits. Akhil is my son. He is the boss here. Change your attitude towards the whole thing. No one is touching your show; it stays as it is.'

By now I was too agitated to care what I was doing. In a fit of pure rage I yelled, 'To hell with the show!' With that I stormed out of the office, slamming the door behind me.

I just couldn't believe they had treated me this shabbily, after I had helped them set up the channel.

I met Yash outside his office, actually my office. He had either heard the raised voices or his father had called him immediately, 'Raghu, stop this. Firstly, no one speaks to dad like that and secondly, if you walk out now there is no coming back.'

'Fuck you and your family business.'

With that I stormed out of office. I was fuming and had no idea where I was going. My mind had just stopped working.

I had gone some paces from the front gate when a white Alto brushed passed me and into the gate. The next moment I heard running footsteps behind me and turned to see Andy.

'Where are you going Raghu? What's wrong? I had dropped by to see you. Apeksha told me you had joined office today. I hadn't got time to visit you when you were home recovering so I thought I would drop by.'

'Leave me alone Andy. I just want to be alone,' I snapped at him.

'No… You stop and tell me what happened,' saying so, he stood in front of me and held my hand to stop me from moving ahead.

'I just had a fight with those bastards. And I am out of Glitterati. It's over.'

'Raghu, you can't fight with everyone like that. Who did you fight with? The father or the son?'

'Both.'

'Come with me. Let's talk about this calmly. Tell me what happened.'

'Andy, it's over,' I shouted. 'They told me if I walked out I would be out forever. And I was mad enough to ask them to fuck off before I walked out.'

'Oh my God!'

'Yes Andy…and I think that you should not be seen with me or they would blacklist you too. So just go,' I was now literally shouting on the road.

I finally convinced Andy to leave and he did so most unwillingly. I was at least glad that at this moment when I had kicked aside the carpet under my feet, I still had friends who cared.

I was now regretting my earlier behaviour. Why did I have to lose my temper?

I dialled Rajeev. Talking to him would surely calm down my nerves.

'Hey Raghu!' Rajeev answered in his usual good-humoured way.

'Can we meet now?'

If he was surprised, he did not show it, 'Come over to my house. We can go down and chat at a coffee shop. Is everything okay Raghu?'

'No, nothing is okay,' I responded, fear and apprehension choking my voice.

'Oh my God! Call me when you reach and I will meet you downstairs.'

I was torn between despair and repentance on my journey to Rajeev's home in Worli. By the time we had chosen a quiet corner at Café Coffee Day, I was dying to tell Rajeev all that had gone wrong.

Rajeev preempted me, 'What happened dude? You seem to be falling into trouble quite often.'

'Yes and this time it's bad.'

'How bad?'

'I asked Singhania and his sons to fuck off and then walked out of the office.'

'WHAT? Are you bloody insane? Raghu you know what this means right? You may lose out on your credibility if word gets out about this.'

'Shit! I should have controlled my temper. But what they were planning for me, my career, was absolutely wrong.'

I told him everything that happened a short while ago.

'Raghu, wrongs things happen to everyone. You are not the only one. And people don't use abusive language and walk out on jobs. That too people at such high posts don't behave like that.'

'Shit! What do I do?' Every second of that episode was now coming back to me in painful detail.

'How angry were they when you left?' asked Rajeev, perhaps trying to gauge how bad the scene was actually.

'Yash said, "If you walk out, it's over!" And I walked out.'

'This can get bad. Just apologise to them and say that you regret your behaviour and losing your temper.'

'Should I call them or text them?' I wanted to do this right.

'Send a text as a sincere apology, to both, and then leave it for the night.'

Rajeev typed out a polite text for me since he was much better at being polite than I was.

It read… '*Dear Mr Singhania. I apologise for my inappropriate behaviour. I deeply regret what I said. I would like to meet you and apologise in person.*'

A similar text was drafted and sent to Yash.

'Fuck! What if they don't reply,' I asked, by now I had bitten off my nails almost upto the nail beds.

'Relax! What you did was wrong, now have the patience to at least wait. You are impossible Raghu! Are you the same young guy who had walked into my office asking for a job? What has happened to you? It's been a long journey for you; you are a self-made man. And this is how you kick everything away—in one shot. All because you have an ego that is almost as bad as your temper? You have to do some introspection and work on your temper,' Rajeev went on to give me a long lecture and I listened quietly because I knew that he was right and I was wrong.

An hour went by, during which I emptied several cups of coffee. But there was no reply, either from the father or the son.

'It's over,' I told myself.

Rajeev showed some sympathy now, after all the badgering, 'Raghu, go home! Try and get some sleep. We will talk tomorrow morning. There is not much we can do now. And don't worry. I will help you as much as I can with this.'

He walked me to my car.

Thoughts ran riot in my head during the drive home. How will my family react? They too will chastise me for my behaviour. Perhaps I should not say all this at home; just say that the Singhanias are cutting down staff because the channel was not doing well—only the top management was being asked to leave because that will save the company more money.

Yes, that sounded much better than the truth.

I checked my phone again to see if there were any messages or missed call from the owners or from office… there were none.

I finally reached home. Apeksha was in Delhi for some national tourism conference. It was late so everyone was asleep. I went to my room and literally crashed onto my bed.

Sleep however was cut short by a nightmare that months had gone by and I was unable to find a job. I woke up with a start and rushed to the washroom to splash water on my face.

I looked into the mirror and read the lines of worry on my reflection. What if this nightmare turned true? What if no one offered me a job? What would I do then? I only had questions…no answers.

Pepper was sleeping peacefully on the bed. I patted him and he opened his eyes to look at me, stretched himself and then put his head on my lap.

I checked my phone again; what if I had missed a call from my employers? No such luck! Should I call Yash or Singhania Senior in the morning? Should I just go to the office? What if I am not allowed in or worse, asked to leave? Obviously I was expecting the worst.

I fell asleep at some point.

I woke up early. Mom was making tea and Reena, reading the newspaper. I picked up a newspaper and sat on the couch.

As usual, my sister was most active in the mornings, 'What's up?'

'Nothing. My head is hurting, so I may just bunk office today.'

'Are you in school that you are making excuses to bunk? Eat something, take a pill and move your ass.'

'No, it's a bad migraine, I guess.'

'Whatever dude! I am getting ready. I have some meetings.'

Thank God she was off; no one else would ask me so many questions.

'Should I give you a head massage?' mom offered.

'No mom, I have some work; need to send a lot of mails so I'm just going inside for an hour or two. I may take a nap then, so will see you in a bit, what are you making for lunch?'

'If you are home I can't make *palak* of course,' she responded with a smile.

'Yes, please don't spoil my one day at home, make some kind of *aloo* and *roti*.'

I walked to my room and shut the door to call Rajeev.

'Hey! How are you?' he asked.

'Not too good… Haven't slept well, had a nightmare that I was jobless for months. Now I am just chilling at home. They didn't reply to my message. Obviously they are still angry.'

'You want me to talk to Yash?' Rajeev asked, as he would often meet Yash in his social circle.

'If you think you can, that will be great. At least I will know what they have decided because now I have no idea what's happening at that end.'

'Okay, let me try speaking to him. I will call you back.'

I waited for Rajeev to call back; pacing my room as I did so. I stopped occasionally to stare out of the window. My house faced the highway. People were going to work, waiting at the bus stop, cars were speeding down the road to reach their respective destinations and I was home. I almost kicked myself.

As I sat down, Pepper was back on my lap. He wanted to be patted and loved. I stroked his head and told myself, at least he loved me with or without any job—no questions asked.

Rajeev called back in half an hour.

'Hello! What happened? Did you speak to him?'

'Yes I did. He was very upset and angry; not so much because you walked out on him, but because you yelled at his father. I made up a story to support you. I told him, "*Yaar* we are all friends. Raghu is going through some personal crisis at home. He is just too stressed. Obviously, he shouldn't have done this but… I thought I should just let you know." He told me that even if he could be convinced, his father won't be, because in the 45 years of senior Singhania's work life, no one had ever walked out like that.'

I had screwed up big time!

'They have kind of made up their mind so there is no going back there Raghu. I am sorry but now the only option would be to quickly plan your next move. We are almost hitting an economic recession and there are very few jobs in the media business. Companies are cutting down staff. You know the scene outside, so I don't really have to tell you that. I will talk to my channel but I don't know which post to even pitch for. Singhania gave you the top post which will be difficult to get now. But what's more important is to get back in the market.'

'Fuck man!'

'Stop fucking and start tapping all your contacts. I will do that too. Meet me in the evening and we will discuss what can be done. Don't worry. I am sure something will come up.'

I knew that Rajeev was being optimistic; the tunnel ahead was a long dark one. The only way was to walk till I could see some light.

I decided that there would be no communication with my team at Glitterati. If anyone called, I was just going to text back saying I was unwell or on a holiday.

The fact that no one had called meant that they had been told that I was out. A few friends called later in the day, but I just let my phone ring.

I had met a few top businessmen; those who had at some point shown interest in getting into the news business through magazines. The line that I was using with them was, '*Hey! I was close to your office. If you are around I will come and say hello*.'

'Sure, you are most welcome,' was the usual answer. Little did they know about my latest fiasco.

During one such meeting I found myself sitting with business tycoon Dhanraj Chavan's son, Dheeraj Chavan, at his South Mumbai office, facing the Queen's Necklace. 'No Raghu. We have no plans to expand. The market is really bad and budgets are very tight. Some investors have backed off so we are just about managing our business this year. Let's see if we can do it next year if the market improves; if things go well we may think of some media venture. I hear even the media business is not good. How is your channel doing?'

'Huh... You are...right. It's not doing great businesswise,' I fumbled and tried to be as convincing as I could.

'Just because I sit inside these four walls doesn't mean I don't know what's happening outside,' the Chavan scion mocked. 'Let's have a glass of whiskey.'

'Yeah sure.'

Dheeraj loved his drinks. He had a state-of-the-art bar in this huge 2000 sq ft private office, facing the Arabian Sea.

'Are you okay with Jack Daniel's?'

'Yes, I love JD.'

'Now tell me how is Singhania doing? I hear his hotels in Goa and Delhi are shutting down. He has been wanting to sell them for over six months now, but no one was ready to buy them.'

I was taken aback, 'Really? I haven't heard about this.'

Dheeraj laughed aloud and said, 'Ask me! I know all the real stories behind the Armani suits. His stupid sons just keep buying cars and are in the news for stupid reasons. Old man is under major stress.'

I was quite amused! From Bollywood gossip I was now sitting with a businessman and discussing gossip about the world of business. We chatted for an hour before I left his office.

I was so used to having people around me that this phase was giving me a feeling of emptiness. Every evening I made some plans with a jobless set of friends to go pub hopping.

Mom did wonder sometimes how I had so much free time suddenly and so many late nights. But I kept making up some stories and managed to convince her each time. Apeksha travelled a lot and was too busy to find out what was happening in my life. When she did I was quick in cooking up stories. I had been in the *make-believe* world for too long.

A regular at pubs and discs in Mumbai would know that brawls are common. One evening, around midnight, when we were happy and high at the Red Light Bar in Sobo, we noticed some guys at a nearby table making cheap gestures at some of our female friends.

We complained to the manager but it was of no use.

After a guy flung a crumpled tissue paper on our table, I got up to confront them.

My opponent was hefty and stood up and pushed me. In a fit of rage, I pushed him back and smashed a bottle on his face. The fight went crazy and soon we found ourselves at the nearby police station. After an hour, we were allowed to make some calls, but I didn't call anyone because I just wanted to get out of this without anyone learning about it.

Though I was a popular face on television, clearly the cops didn't watch English channels, so they never recognised me. I have noticed that there are always situations where a set of people will spot you immediately. And then…there are those where you would be a nobody.

My friend's father had to pay Rs 50,000 for all of us and we were allowed to leave. His father screamed at him, right in front of us, 'Stop hanging out with these useless boys. This is the last time I am getting you out of trouble. Stop this or learn to clean your own mess.'

I couldn't believe that I had actually got into a pub brawl. Such things happened during college years. Not with someone who had almost been a celebrity.

I reached home late in the night with bruises on my face. Thankfully, everyone was asleep and Apeksha was out of town. I washed my face and cleaned the wounds as much as I could.

The next morning when my mom and sister noticed, I made up a story that I fell from a friend's bike, but even that got them worried.

Mom asked, 'Did you get hurt anywhere else? Are you okay? Want to go to a doctor?'

'No mom, I am fine,' I assured her.

I felt like I was hitting a dead end with my professional life and now I was ashamed that I had got involved in a brawl. I decided to meet Rajeev in the evening. Thank God for a friend like him, I wouldn't have known what to do otherwise.

Rajeev was horrified when I told him what happened the night before and he warned me to stay out of such trouble.

'Raghu, why are you doing this? What if they were sons of some politicians, somebody with connections in high places? Who would get you out of the mess then? Think of your family before doing such things. And you are in enough trouble already with respect to your career. Do you want your name to appear on television channels as *Raghu Reporter was taken away in handcuffs*? Do you think you will get a job with anybody afer that?'

Rajeev and I again discussed about my future but couldn't come up with a concrete plan. I had to wait patiently for something to click.

While driving back I was caught at a police *nakabandi* and since I had had two drinks I was charged for drunken driving. My license was taken away and I had to spend the night in a lockup. I was allowed to leave only after being produced in the local court the next morning.

As the charges were being read out, I just prayed that some reporter would not recognise me. Courtrooms are favourite haunts of small time reporters looking for sensational tidbits to ensure some good sales of their respective newspapers.

I hadn't had the guts to inform my family or even Rajeev. I just called my mom to tell her that I was at a party so would spend the night at a friend's place instead of driving late.

A night in jail and then morning at the court. Could things get any worse!

20

Back in the Game

Apeksha was away for a week now. We talked on the phone everyday; she asked me about work and I lied to her. I hated it but I had decided to explain everything to her face to face. She would be home next week.

The kind of people I met these days offered me a drink everytime, no matter what time of the day it was. And for some reason I could never refuse. I had no office to go to and not many knew that.

Last few times when Rajeev called I was in high spirits, literally. As a good friend he warned me of the consequences of not cutting down and asked me to focus. So, I made sure that I didn't touch alcohol when I was with him. I had lost faith in myself but Rajeev hadn't. I should have considered myself lucky.

He knew the owners of News Asian TV and had spoken to them about me and even lined up a meeting for me at 10 a.m. at Nariman Point.

The night before the meeting was to happen, I was at one of my, now common, drinking sessions. So the morning of the interview I woke up at 9 a.m. with a terrible hangover. I even threw up a couple of times. Realising that I was running late I only had time to wash my face, get into a suit and rush out.

'We have to reach Nariman Point in half an hour! Anyhow!' I instructed my driver as I got into the car.

Mom had given me some biscuits for the drive. I ate the biscuits, drank water before taking a tablet, and made a great effort to keep all that inside. I repeatedly told myself that I should not have had alcohol last night when I knew I had an important meeting in the morning. I frantically looked at my watch every couple of minutes as the car crawled alongside the office-going traffic.

Fifteen minutes into the drive I realised that I would definitely not make it on time. So I decided that once I crossed Dadar I would call the secretary (whose number Rajeev had given me after making the appointment) and inform her that I was running 15-20 minutes late because of the terrible traffic. Unfortunately for me it was the day Anna Hazare had his rally at Azad Maidan. So there was a crazy traffic jam in South Mumbai. So I was technically not lying.

I reached half an hour late and was relieved to learn that Harsh Juneja, one of the investors of News Asian TV was also running late. I was introduced to the Editor-in-Chief, Lee Gong, who was based out of Singapore.

'Hello Raghu, I have heard so much about you. In fact you are quite popular in Singapore; people associate Bollywood with you.'

'Thank you so much Lee.'

Lee was friendly and forthcoming and I liked him immediately. We chatted about the entertainment business for half an hour and then Harsh Juneja joined us.

'Hello Raghu. Welcome. Sorry, I am late.' Immaculately dressed in a business suit he seemed to be cut out of the same cloth as the senior Singhania.

In my mind, I thanked him for being late. But the headache had increased. Unlike my meetings these days, I held a cup of black coffee, and not whiskey, and it was gradually showing me its benefits.

'Not a problem Mr Juneja, in fact, I was having a nice chat with Lee.'

'That's nice! Okay Raghu, I am going to keep this short and I hope this stays between us.'

He continued, 'Singhania and I know each other well. We had once decided that we will never exchange staff. Of course, this cannot be completely avoided at junior level, which we don't really care about, but like say at your level, if I take you away from Singhania it will be like breaking a promise. What you have to do is, quit that job and then join us after a month or so. I can at least say that I picked you from the market once you had left his company. I don't want to blatantly break an understanding.'

Lee took over, 'Now about your job profile... See, the difference is we are not an entertainment channel. We are a news channel and for us entertainment is an important beat, like sports, business, crime, city etc. You can head the entertainment beat but the exposure is going to be less than what you currently have at Glitterati.'

'Hmm... I get it,' I pretended that I was actually weighing the pros and cons of this eventuality.

Juneja added, 'I want quality people and Rajeev Mehra, who is a dear friend, mentioned you. I thought we should meet and take it ahead if you wish to do it the way I told you. Another important aspect is that your package will be slightly less because your work will be less too. You just have to focus on your shows and the beat in general. The channel in general is doing very well. Our channel also has an international audience, so the reach is very good.'

With this Juneja got up, walked towards me and shook my hand, 'Think about it for a few days and get back to Lee or me. I will take your leave now...' Since I was down in the dumps I didn't care if I sounded desperate, 'No sir, wait... I have thought about it. I would like to take it up. I will do it the way you ask.'

Juneja sat down, 'Are you sure?'

'Yes I am. Because I always wanted to work with an international channel and this is the perfect opportunity for me.'

'So let's shake hands over this. Let me know when you are out of Singhania's camp completely.'

Oh my God! I am back! Am I back? I couldn't believe that I was actually back in the running. I called Rajeev and told him all about the meeting. The only thing we feared was them finding out about my episode with the Singhanias. 'If the Singhanias say anything I will just say that they are lying because I have decided to move on. I really have no option Rajeev,' I declared.

'I guess that would be the best way to handle this. Raghu, this is a good opportunity, please please, make this work. Keep your cool always. To be in the business you have to swallow your pride a lot of times. We all do that. If you want to be in the business then you have to follow the same.'

'I understand Rajeev. I can't thank you enough. Let's meet for dinner. My treat.'

We opened a bottle of champagne at the restaurant later in the evening.

'Please don't say "Fuck Off" to Harsh Juneja ever. He will bump you off. He is more influential than the Singhanias.'

'No, no! No more *Fucking Off* anyone.' I raised my glass as a promise and the two of us burst out laughing.

'Yes. If you do, then rest assured you definitely have to fuck off from the country,' Rajeev said, when he had stopped laughing.

Apeksha was going to return to Mumbai by the late night flight. I had decided that I would tell her *about* the switch, but not *why*.

We wrapped up the celebrations early. I had a driver today to take me to the airport. I didn't want to take the risk of landing up in the lockup again and my wife having to bail me out.

As Apeksha walked out of the airport, we hugged each other. We were meeting after two weeks, 'Sorry darling, this was a long trip. After the conference, I had to shoot my show at Jaipur during the literary fest. I am so exhausted.'

As we drove out of the airport, Apeksha asked, 'How is Pepper doing? Mom said that he has been unwell.'

'Yes, she took him to the vet. He is better now.'

'I can't wait to see him.'

She held my hand, 'I missed you. What have you been upto. How has Mumbai treated you in my absence?'

I wish I could tell her truthfully how the city had thrashed me around for the past few days; losing my job, brawl at a pub, night in a lockup, drinking binges... But I kept all of that to myself, as I had decided.

'How do you think I would be, when I was missing you terribly?' I responded finally.

She smiled and held my hand tighter.

Back home, mom and Reena were all ears about Apeksha's trip. Pepper too sat at Apeksha's feet, as though listening to the stories about the city, the shooting, the event. However unlike my mom and sister, he got bored very soon and dozed off.

In the early hours of the morning, when Apeksha and I were in our room, I told her all about the most important development in my life... Well, not all.

'I am moving on from Glitterati.'

'What!' She almost shouted.

'Relax, I will tell you everything. The Singhanias are not doing well in their business. Their hotels are shutting and they are going bankrupt. I have got a great offer from News Asian TV which is an international channel.'

I paused to see her reaction. But she was just looking at me, wide-eyed. I continued, 'I met Juneja. It's a yes from his side. Work will be less which is what I prefer right now. And yes, the package will also be slightly lesser than Glitterati.'

'The offer is good because they have an international audience, but request them to match your current package. You are one of the most popular faces in film journalism.'

'See, I have always told you that given an option I would love to live abroad but because of my contacts in this stupid world of Bollywood I am stuck in India. Now this could be the first step to go international and maybe an opportunity will arise to live abroad. Bollywood is big in the US and the UK.'

I listed out the other factors that I had identified as advantages of this new job and that finally assured her that this was indeed a good move. But she still insisted that I re-negotiate my package.

After two days, I called Lee and told him that I had put in my papers and wouldn't need to serve any notice. So I could join at the earliest.

'This is great news Raghu. I will talk to Mr Juneja and someone from the management will call you and get the paperwork going so that we can complete all the necessary formalities.'

Inspite of the assurance from Harsh Juneja and Lee, I lived the days, leading up to my receiving the appointment letter, with some amount of trepidation. I had told Apeksha too that I would not have to serve the requisite one month notice period. This had helped to explain why I now spent so many days at home before I took on my new responsibility. Of course, I hadn't told her that I was yet to receive my appointment letter.

In a week's time the paperwork was done and I joined News Asian TV as the Managing Editor, Entertainment. The social media was abuzz with this news and that included the news portals. Some business reporters who worked for the web called me for my quotes.

I had memorised just one response for this eventuality. 'It was time to move on. I am now looking forward to catering to an international audience.'

I was lucky that the Singhanias had not made the episode of our altercation public. So, no one knew about the short break I was forced to take.

Soon I found myself inundated with messages from actors and producers wishing me luck for my change.

I was back! The nightmare thankfully had not lasted long.

The biggest lesson I had learnt was not to lose my cool. Ever! Whatever happens I would never ask any boss to *fuck off*.

21

Wrong Place. Wrong Time.

News Asian TV had its editorial office in Bandra, which completely worked for me because Chembur to Bandra is just seven kms and in a city like Mumbai, that was a fairly sensible distance to cover, everyday, for work.

My weekend show, *Rendezvous with Raghu Kumar* was soon to go on air. Based on an informal format, it would be more news-heavy. It was still a celebrity interview but not confined to a studio and we were more concerned with finding out what a celebrity was currently upto. So, say actor Aamir Khan met social activist Anna Hazare, we will do an interview with him talking about social issues. The informal setting immediately caught the imagination of the audience. We interviewed the celebrities in small cafés and restaurants and even at tea stalls. People were clearly bored with the studio format so we decided to step out and give it a good visual treatment.

News Asian TV slotted my show at the exact same time as Akhil Singhania's show, *One on One with Akhil Singhania* on Glitterati. It had the same old studio format.

Because of my rapport with the actors, the new format and the reach of the channel, which was supported by a great marketing team, *Rendezvous* was way ahead of Akhil's show. When the TRP's started showing this over consecutive Fridays, it raised quite a storm with the Singhanias. I found out through my old contacts in the channel that Akhil had started to tell people how I was kicked out of the channel because of my unprofessional attitude.

I knew that if the story went around for too long and if too many people spoke about it then some might even start believing it. I had to clear the air before things got nastier. A lot of time had passed since the incident so I sent a text to Raj Kumar Singhania, requesting for a meeting.

He was a big man with a big heart and we did share a great rapport at one point and since I had learnt that Yash was out of the country, this was a good time to approach him. Singhania senior immediately replied agreeing to meet me. His text read, '*Come over to my office...*'

It was agreed that I would go over to his office at 3 p.m. the next day.

'I can't believe that he agreed to meet you after all that happened.' Rajeev was quite surprised when I told him. Now I made it a point to inform him every time I wanted to do anything too adventurous.

'But what are you going to tell him? What is this meeting for?'

'I just want to break the ice with him. I am not going to bring up anything; be very polite, so that he feels compelled to ask Akhil to back off and stop what he is doing.'

'Sounds good. But watch your words. Remember the last time you were there you spoke like an idiot and got yourself into trouble,' Rajeev warned.

I reached the Glitterati office. It was a nostalgic feeling driving through the tall gates.

Shaila still worked as the receptionist and was happy to see me.

'How are you sir? So nice to see you. We really miss you. Are you coming back sir?'

'No, I am not coming back, dear. I am hear to see the Senior. I have an appointment at 3 p.m.'

That was the nickname the employees had for Raj Kumar Singhania—Senior or Daddy.

'You can go straight up. He is already in his office.'

'Thanks Shaila…and you still have the best smile in this office.'

She blushed. Singhania senior had a new personal assistant, I noticed.

'Hi, I am Raghu.'

'Of course I know you. Sir told me you will be here at dot three. He said you are very punctual.'

She led me to the newly renovated office. I had learnt that the office interiors was being done up according to *Vaastu*, as Senior was a firm believer.

'Raghu! Welcome! Should I be scared because the last time you were here you had asked my show and me to go to hell,' he laughed.

'Sir please, don't embarrass me anymore. I really feel terrible remembering that incident.'

'I am just joking. In business we can't fight about these stupid things. We all have to let go. I am happy that you are doing well with my friend Juneja.'

'Sir you are what you are because of your benevolence. The day I begin to think like you, I will be a happy man.'

'You were my favourite Raghu and you know that. Now that you are sitting here again, let's have a glass of wine.'

'Sure sir, it would be my pleasure.'

He walked over to the bar and poured me some red wine, and said, 'This is one of the finest wines that my friend sends me from France. Whenever my supply goes down, I just have to send him a mail and he sends me 10 bottles each time.'

'Wow! You must introduce me to him. I wouldn't mind receiving one bottle each month...'

Singhania had a rich man's laughter. I mean, whatever people might say about his business doing badly, one could see that he was a happy man. When you sat with him he didn't gossip about anyone or talk people down. He was like a King—larger than life, somebody one would aspire to be like some day. 'You know Raghu, when I was your age, I was restless too. I wanted success very fast, but time and experience of the world teaches you to slow down. Nothing is going to run away, so we all should take it easy. The only thing that will run out of our grasp will be our lives and till we have that we should make the best of it.'

I knew that this *gyaan* was definitely going to be useful in the long run. 'Where is Yash? How is he doing?' I asked.

'He has gone to Dubai to sell some of our shows to a local channel there. I wonder how he will react if he finds out you are here. He is hot-headed like you. I don't blame both of you—you are still young. *Life sikha degi tum dono ko kab aur kitna brake lagana hai.* (Life will teach you when and how to slow down.)'

Singhania had a habit of walking while he talked.

I watched as he stood at his window, staring out at the sea. He finished his glass of wine and the next thing I knew he had fallen flat on the floor.

I ran to hold him shouting, 'Sir, Sir, are you okay?'

Hearing me, his personal assistant came running inside.

'Oh my God! What happened?'

'I don't know. He was having wine and looking out of the window and then suddenly he just fell on the floor.' I checked his pulse and his heartbeat as she called the ambulance.

I felt a wave of panic rise inside me. Why did these things have to happen to me?

Akhil ran in and seeing me, started yelling, as expected, 'What are you doing here? What happened to my dad? What did you do?'

'Akhil, calm down,' I said, although I was feeling anything but calm inside. 'I was here to meet him. He called me. We were chatting and he just collapsed.'

'Did you argue with him? What did you tell him?'

'We didn't have any argument,' I said in exasperation, as he bombarded me with accusations.

Akhil caught me by the collar and pushed me to the wall saying, 'If anything happens to my dad…you are fucking dead.'

The ambulance arrived and senior Singhania was carried into it. Akhil pushed me aside as I attempted to climb into the ambulance. I had thought it was my duty to be at the hospital in case the doctor had questions about how he had been minutes before the collapse.

By now there was a lot of commotion in the office; the staff was standing out. Most of them were making calls.

I got into my car to go to the hospital. Just then my phone rang—it was an international number.

'You bastard, what were you doing in my office? What did you do to my dad? Did you poison him? Let me come back, you are going to spend the rest of your life in jail.'

It was Yash and before I could say anything he had hung up.

I reached Breach Candy Hospital to realise that Akhil had already called the cops.

Pointing at me, he said, 'Inspector, he was the one with my dad when this happened.'

I was asked to sit in the police van and my phones were taken away. I was to be taken to the police station.

I realised there was no point panicking, 'Sir I want to call my laywer. I am a reporter.'

The inspector responded, 'We know you. But today you have done a big thing. If you want to call your lawyer, then do so once we reach the police station.'

Fuck! I just held my head and sat down quietly. This time I didn't even do anything. I don't know why I visited Singhania. I should have just let his stupid son spread the stories and I could have just denied everything. I was just at the wrong place at the wrong time.

The word spread and Rajeev and Apeksha came to the police station with a lawyer, late in the evening, to bail me out.

Apeksha just looked stunned. Rajeev spoke out first, 'What happenned Raghu? Tell us everything. This is breaking news. Some channels are showing visuals of you being taken into a police van.'

'Nothing happened. I was having a nice chat with Singhania. He was drinking wine and looking outside the window and then suddenly he collapsed. That's it. I don't even know if it was a heart attack or something else.'

'Did you have the wine?' Apeksha asked as she drove through the busy traffic.

'No! In fact he was praising this wine which some friend of his sends from France…and I was listening to him…and then…'

Rajeev tried to put my mind at rest. 'If that is what happened it will soon come out in the open. This was nothing but a knee jerk reaction of the sons; blame the person who was there.'

Back home, I turned on the television. There were speculations galore about the episode. I quickly moved on from those channels. News 25 had done a phone interview with Yash as he was boarding the flight to Mumbai. It was being played repeatedly, 'The last time Raghu walked out of our office was after a bad fight. I don't understand why he returned to meet my dad. Police will make him talk.'

'You fought with the Singhanias and left? Why is Yash saying all this?' Apeksha looked at me in horror as she put the TV on mute.

'He is just bullshitting. He talks crap each time he opens his mouth.'

The doorbell rang. It was the watchman. '*Madam, woh bahut TV camerawale aaye hain bahar. Saab se milna hai keh rahe hain.* (Madam, several TV camera guys are here. They all want to meet sir.)'

Apeksha immediately called Vishal Thadani, our family friend and lawyer, 'You have to come here. The media guys are here. Unless you give them a sound byte they will not leave. Better to get this done now.'

As a journalist she knew the importance of an official statement.

Thadani promised to be at our place in half an hour.

Apeksha instructed the watchman to tell the reporters that we would talk to the media in the presence of our lawyer only; which was in another half an hour.

While returning from the police station I had called Harsh Juneja to tell him all that had happened. He of course was curious about why I had gone to meet Raj Kumar Singhania. I assured him that it was only a courtesy visit to a former employer because I shared a cordial relationship with him. He only wanted to know how I was doing in my new job. Juneja had assured me that he would stand by me through this episode.

The lawyer arrived and addressed the media, stating the episode as it had happened, adding that there was no foul play as the sons were suggesting.

'If they check the CCTV, which is in every room and corridor of that building, they will see that we were just having a nice chat. His sons, of course, will not do something this sensible. They only want to throw accusations,' I said in exasperation, as we were discussing what should be the next course of action.

'That's it,' said Apeksha with a smile. 'Mr Thadani, this will definitely clear Raghu's name.'

'I will immediately file an application saying that the police should take the recorded CCTV footage right away. We need to do this at the earliest before Yash or Akhil tamper with it to suit their own ends.'

I agreed, 'I don't trust those fu***rs at all.'

'Calm down Raghu,' said Apeksha.

My mom and sister were really worried and mute spectators to the circus around them. But they trusted Apeksha and Mr Thadani, our lawyer, to handle this well. Dogs are very perceptive and so Pepper could sense that I was troubled. When I was sitting alone late in the night—Rajeev and Mr Thadani had left and the others were in their respective rooms—he came and rested his head on my lap. Stroking his head, as I wondered about what now lay ahead, was actually quite therapeutic.

Life presents the strangest of challenges. From a nobody I had risen to become a celebrity reporter and now a quirk of fate had made me a criminal in the eyes of the country, before I was to be exonerated.

I found myself joining a queue of accused as we waited for our respective case to be called out.

The day of the court hearing had come sooner than expected.

'What did you do?' the man behind me asked.

I had no intentions of chatting up with the common thieves and criminals around me. But the man repeated his question.

'Nothing! They have made a false case against me.'

Out of curiosity I asked him what he was there for. 'Some local boys used to tease my sister. I told them a few times to leave her alone, but they didn't listen to me. I stabbed and killed one.'

'Oh! Ok.'

'Do you see that man in front of you. The one in the white *kurta*?'

'Who is he?' I asked.

'He is the Don of Sanpada, Babu Bhai.'

I had heard of Babu Bhai, I mean everyone in Mumbai had, but I was seeing him in such close proximity, for the first time.

My eyes happened to wander to Apeksha and her expression told me that I should now stop bonding with the criminals, as my case would be announced soon and the judge shouldn't see me having a good time and chatting up the who's who of the crime world.

'Case number 12, Singhania v/s Kumar,' the court attendant called out.

Mr Thadani passed all the legal papers to the judge who slowly read through every page. It also included a bail extension application, in case the case continued for a long time.

The judge asked the police to submit the CCTV footage to the court before 5 p.m. that evening and also submit a report of the recording.

'Since bail has been granted for three days, extension will be decided only at the end of that period. Next hearing would be tomorrow at 10 a.m,' the judge said, striking his gavel.

As I walked out with my family, I asked Mr Thadani if I would have to come to court everyday. He assured me that I would have to do that in the early days of the case and joked that that was because the judges too got tired of seeing the same faces of the lawyers. They too wanted to see new faces.

Rajeev had an important interview with Karan Johar and had to rush to work immediately, assuring me that he would stay in touch and that I should not get worried, for things would be cleared very soon.

My family once again reminded me how lucky I was to have a friend like Rajeev.

'Very few people get such friends in life,' mom said.

I spent the day at home. Apeksha had also taken the day off and so had Reena. So we spent some really quality time together as a family—a rare occasion. I just wished that the circumstances that brought this about were different. The mood was sombre, but we tried to make each other smile. Pepper was the only one who was happy, without any reservations. He was glad to have all of us together and spent most of the day running around and playing with his ball, which he wanted us to throw so that he could fetch it from the farthest end of the room.

Rajeev called me that night, 'A lot of actors have called me to ask what happened.'

'This is so embarrassing Rajeev, for all these people to know that I am involved in this case. Even if a few people believe that I did something to Raj Kumar Singhania, that will be really harmful for my career.'

'Oh come on! No one is going to believe that you wanted to kill the old man. And most of them are asking because they are concerned. You have a lot of goodwill Raghu, you will come out of this soon.'

'It's funny *na* how many times I have got into trouble. And each time you have stood by me.'

'Come on, this is not your fault. Relax and get some sleep.'

'Thanks, you know I always regretted saying *"Fuck off"* and walking out of the office, but now I am so glad I said it to Yash's face.'

Rajeev laughed aloud, 'You are mad Raghu! At such a time you can think of this!'

'Good night.'

'Night dude! Take care.'

Later, I told Apeksha, 'You can go to work if you want. God knows how many days this stupid hearing will go on. All I have to do is go to the court and Mr Thadani anyway has to accompany me.'

'No no, I will come with you. I have worked very hard in the last few weeks so taking it easy for a few days will do no damage.'

Next day, Apeksha and Reena came with me to the court.

Rajeev couldn't make it because he was leaving for the US for an interview with Daniel Craig for his latest Bond film.

At 10 a.m. our names were again called out. No one was there from Singhania's side because the old man was in the hospital. His laywer asked for rejection of my bail with immediate effect.

The judge responded, 'The CCTV recordings clearly show that there was no altercation between Raj Kumar Singhania and Raghu Kumar; in fact it shows that they were just talking. Mr Singhania poured wine for the accused and himself and collapsed after he had finished the contents of his glass.'

Mr Thadani in my defence argued, 'Your honour, here is the text message exchange between Raghu Kumar and Raj Kumar Singhania which proves that Mr Singhania gave an appointment to Mr Kumar. And this is a copy of the statement of his personal secretary, who says that there was no fight. Please note that her workstation is right outside the door. Here is Mr Singhania's latest health report which shows that he has very high sugar. There is reason to believe that his sugar shot up because of the glass of wine. He fell because of health complications—there was no foul play. And both his sons, who are alleging foul play, were not even present for this meeting; in fact Yash was not even in the country. It's just suspicion. There is no basis to prove their accusations.'

Accepting all of Mr Thadani's arguments, the judge let me off and closed the case. There was absolutely nothing to prove me guilty.

I could see Apeksha and Reena hug each other in relief.

'I can't believe Yash was so dumb to have dragged me to the court without any evidence. Once an idiot always an idiot,' I said as my sister and wife came and hugged me.

I asked Mr Thadani, 'How did you get Singhania's medical report?'

'If there is a case going on, hospitals are obligated to hand over the reports if a lawyer asks for them. Hospitals have legal departments for this and this is anyway a regular procedure.'

'Wow! I didn't know that, I learnt something new today. Might come handy someday.'

'And you nearly paid a damn heavy price for this small lesson man,' my sister said with a laugh.

'We could sue them and claim damages for trying to ruin your reputation,' Mr Thadani suggested.

'No, Mr Thadani, I am tired. I just want to get back to work.'

22

The Big Party

Harsh Juneja threw a party for me at Mumbai's Taj Mahal Hotel the very next day. A few senior colleagues and my family and friends were invited. Everyone welcomed me back from the horrific experience that could have ended my career, not to mention pushed me behind bars. The incident, as expected, had made headlines. After all, we lived in the breaking news age. Every news is breaking news! Every update is also breaking news!

Now that the stage was set and wine was being served I was expected to address the gathering. Since my family and friends were present I didn't mind taking the microphone to thank everyone. Mom, Apeksha, Reena and Rajeev were standing close to the stage.

I was greeted by an applause as I took the microphone.

'First, let me warn you I don't have a prepared speech if you are expecting one!'

A friend shouted out, 'Yes Raghu, we know you are a star reporter and don't have to rely on a prepared speech.'

Everyone laughed at that and thankfully that set the mood for what I wanted to say.

'Right! But I do have a few important things to say here. I am going to take five minutes so I suggest those of you who can spot a chair somewhere around just grab it. It has not been an easy journey since I started. As a child I played the role of a beggar in a movie and that scene was edited out (*my audience laughed aloud*). I so wanted it at that time, but God clearly had better plans for me. If that scene existed, my good friends would have made sure it went viral in today's day and age! I hated Bollywood that day, because my scene was deleted from the movie.

'I got into journalism. Bollywood was the beat I was given, on day one, thanks to Rajeev who is standing right there. That day I also made a friend for life; Rajeev who has supported me through thick and thin. Bollywood is my bread and butter even today. I saw a lot of filth around in the film industry. Stories about marital affairs that made me feel sick at the beginning until my banker uncle cheated on his wife. And here I thought these things happened only in Bollywood. So why do I always blame Bollywood?

'When I was a rookie reporter, I was trapped by a senior journalist into doing a story that was all wrong. It made it on air and I lost my credibility and held onto my job by the skin of my teeth. She was a top Bollywood journalist and once again I found a reason to hate Bollywood. I wondered what kind of people existed in this stupid industry.

'Each time a film star made me wait I used to hate this industry even more; my first big print story on Parveen Babi who was once a top film star, but died alone, made this hatred grow.

'Let me confess something here today, I never wanted to live in India. All my friends knew that I loved the prospect of staying and working in another country; New York,

London, but I got stuck here in India because of my good contacts in the film industry. And then I was doing fairly well so I didn't want to start all over again in a new place. I felt I had got trapped here in India because of Bollywood.

'Each time something went wrong, I blamed Bollywood. Hating this industry had become a habit.

'But now, today, when I stand here, I look back at everything that I have got, everything that I have achieved... It's all thanks to Bollywood! The love, the fame, the money...it's all because of Bollywood. Why did I hate this industry when all that I had experienced here happens in every other industry? The only difference is that when it happens in Bollywood it catches the eye and everyone finds out and talks about it. But Bollywood is nothing but a reflection of the society that we live in. So before I say the line that I never thought I would, I want to thank my mom, my wife, my sister, and Rajeev for being with me through thick and thin and Mr Harsh Juneja for the big opportunity and for this lovely evening.

'So I am going to say this now... just so that it's on record...'

Before I could complete, a loud blast shook the entire hotel and was followed by the sound of gun shots. Almost immediately, there was smoke inside the room and within no time nothing was visible.

Everyone was shouting and frantically looking for their loved ones. I hid behind the stage with Rajeev, Apeksha, Reena and my mom. By now we were all holding hands in terror. What was going on, we wondered.

The hotel staff locked the door of the banquet area where the event was being held, to secure the people inside the room. They were obviously scared too but they took charge and after locking the doors blocked them with heavy tables and chairs.

By this time, people were making and receiving frantic calls. We finally knew that the hotel was under siege and terrorists were roaming the corridors. Since it was the first floor, people pulled down curtains, tied them together to create long ropes, so that we could go down through the emergency exit windows. The hotel staff helped them. Soon the fire engines arrived and the fire fighters put a ladder against the window to help more people. They then rushed the injured to the waiting ambulances for medical attention.

Every few minutes, grenade blasts shook up the entire hotel. It was difficult to even breathe normally as the room was full of smoke; everyone was coughing.

Apeksha, mom and Reena had gone down because the senior citizens, women and children had been asked to go down first. The men were soon helping the hotel staff. Rajeev and I also pitched in. There was much panic all around; an old lady was too scared to get out of the window. We somehow convinced her but she fainted as soon as she reached the window.

Even as people were trying to make their escape through the window there was the sound of banging at the door.

'*Darwaza kholo*!' shouted the terrorists.

When they were unable to break down the door they sprayed it with bullets from their automatic weapons.

By this time I was climbing out of the window and just as Rajeev was about to follow me, the door was broken down by the terrorists.

On realising that people were making their way out of the window, one of them fired at the window and Rajeev got shot on his shoulder.

I was close to the window even though I was outside. I instinctively caught hold of Rajeev's shirt and hauled him down after me. The result was that we both tumbled down and missed the stack of curtains the fire fighters had piled up to cushion any fall. We both were hurt; Rajeev more serious as he had a bullet injury. We both were taken into the same ambulance.

Rajeev was in severe pain, with his wound bleeding severely. The nurse in the ambulance was trying her best to get the wound to stop bleeding.

She told me, '*Aap inse baat karte raho. Inko sone mat dena*! (Keep talking to him. Make sure he does not fall asleep.)'

'Rajeev, you hear that? Look at me. Talk to me,' I shouted intermittently.

His eyes were shut; it was obvious that he was in severe pain. 'Man… Shot… I have been shot!'

I kept talking to him to ensure that he did not fall asleep. The nearest hospital, Cama, was not operational because the terrorists had attacked there as well. We rushed to a nursing home nearby on Marine Drive; here too, it was difficult to manoeuvre the ambulance as the road had been blocked in places by police barricades, which were not allowing cars through. Only ambulances were being allowed. All the hospitals in the vicinity were on high alert.

I called Apeksha and learnt that they were safe at the police headquarters. They had the option of staying there till it was safe to step out.

I told her, 'Do not leave the police headquarters till I come for you; even if it's morning. Rajeev has been hit by a bullet and we are at a nursing home.'

'What!' Apeksha was horrified.

'He had asked me to go out of the window first and those bastards entered the room just as he was about to step out. He was shot; thankfully on his shoulder or he would have died there and then.'

'Oh my God! Does his family know?'

'No, I will be calling them now. I don't know how to tell them.'

'You take care of Rajeev and yourself. I'll talk to his family,' Apeksha offered. 'You are anyway sounding out of breath. They will be more worried. Let me handle this.'

I agreed as Apeksha could handle such situations much better than I did. I asked her to wait till I got the latest update on Rajeev's health. Rajeev had been rushed into the ICU of the nursing home. I had been asked to wait in the reception, after my wounds had been attended to. I sat there along with a group of anxious people, all worried about what was happening in the city. The door of the hospital had been locked to prevent a scenario like the Cama Hospital, where the terrorists had entered. The news reports said that the terrorists were still inside the hotel and on a killing spree.

Realising what we had escaped and wondering about the plight of the others who were still there, I held my head and broke down. The boy at the reception just held me tight, to quell the fear racking my head.

Soon the doctor came out to inform me about Rajeev, 'I have taken the bullet out. He is sleeping now. You can see him from outside, but don't go in, let him sleep.'

The doctor then rushed to attend the steady inflow of patients being brought in by the cops.

I checked on Rajeev. His blood pressure and heart rate were being noted by the monitor. As I looked at him, I realised what a close shave he had had, and was unable to rein in the tears. I sat in the waiting area, having decided to wait till Rajeev woke up. I called Apeksha to update her on Rajeev's condition so she could call his family. The most important thing was to let them know that he was out of danger and sleeping now.

Soon my phone started ringing; it was Rajeev's landline.

'Raghu, where are you? We will be there now.' It was Rajeev's dad.

'Uncle, please calm down. I am with him and he is sleeping. You can't step out of the house now. You know the city is under attack and I am sure a number of roads are closed. The terrorists are apparently all over the place.'

'Those bastards! They shot my son,' he broke down on the phone, requesting me to tell him the truth about Rajeev.

'Uncle, it's the truth. He is out of danger and will be awake soon. You please don't leave home. It is more important that you stay indoors—safe and sound. We would not be able to deal with anything more, so please stay at home.'

'Okay *beta*, call me as soon as he wakes up.'

Soon, a police constable walked in. He wanted to take Rajeev's statement but I told him what the doctor had told me; that Rajeev should not be disturbed. I was keeping a watch on Rajeev's room as the hospital staff was busy attending other patients.

The constable had quite a few questions for me.

'What were you and your friend doing at the Taj Mahal hotel?'

'My boss, Harsh Juneja, had thrown a party for me. I am a film reporter and the person who has been shot is also a film reporter.'

'Did you see the person who shot your friend?'

'No, not clearly.'

'You must have seen something. How many people were there?'

'No, the hall was full of smoke, so it was not possible to see anything.'

'How many people were present at the party and how many went out of the window?

'There were about 50 to 70 people at the party and all of them went down safely. Only Rajeev and I were left; he was the last one, so he got shot as the terrorists broke the door to enter the room.'

'You are saying there were 50 to 70 people in the room and only one got shot?'

'Yes, all of them went out through the window. We were the last ones in the room and when we were getting down, they broke into the room and started firing.'

'Who did you see?'

'God! I didn't see them!'

'Take this paper and pen. Write down the names and numbers of everybody there; whatever you can remember. I will come back soon.'

I wrote down whatever I could remember. My hands trembled as I did that. The constable returned; he was wiping his hands with a handkerchief which, I noticed, had blood stains.

'Whose blood is that?' I asked him, pointing at his hand.

'This is Mumbai's blood,' he responded and I realised how he too must be disturbed; even Mumbai police had never seen such a ghastly attack before.

He took the names and contact numbers from me and before leaving, instructed me to come to the police station once things calmed down to normal to share any leads I might have.

'Thank you sir, you take care of yourself,' I told him.

He left the hospital, alone on his motorcycle—this, irrespective of the fact that the dark streets of Mumbai were now as bad as a war zone. The cop had no life jacket, no companion; in short, no defence in case he was attacked.

I went back to check on Rajeev. He was still sleeping. I noted his heart rate and blood pressure on the monitor.

I fell asleep outside the ICU and was woken up at 4 a.m. to be told that Rajeev had opened his eyes.

I rushed into the room immediately, after the nurse, who was there to check his vitals. 'Raghu, how are you? Where are we?' I realised that he was still in a daze, recovering from the anaesthesia.

'I am fine Rajeev. We are in South Mumbai; at a local nursing home. Do you remember anything that happened?'

'Yes of course I do. But I don't know when I blanked out.'

'You got shot as you were about to step out of the window. I pulled you by your shirt and we both fell down from the first floor.'

'Thanks… My shoulder hurts.'

'Yes, you were hit by a bullet, but it's out now; didn't penetrate too deep, as the doctors say. Thank God for that!'

The nurse interrupted to say that I should let Rajeev sleep.

We just ignored her and started talking once she stepped out.

'Rajeev, if you are feeling upto it, can you talk to your dad. He is really worried.'

'You told him?'

'Yes Rajeev, I had to.'

'Okay, call him fast… My head is hurting…'

It was a short call, because he was still under the influence of medication and exhausted. Assuring Rajeev that I would be around if he wanted anything, I stepped out of the ICU.

I first called Mr Juneja to update him about everything; he had just left the police headquarters and was on his way home. He too had been worried about Rajeev.

'I will keep you posted Mr Juneja. Get home safe.'

'Take care Raghu.'

Few of us in the nursing home lobby continued to watch the news. I felt terrible for the people on the higher floors of the Taj Hotel, who were still stuck in their hotel rooms. We learnt that commando teams had arrived in Mumbai and had taken charge of the situation.

My phone rang. It was Apeksha.

'Hi, we are going home. The police has arranged for a bus with security and they are dropping all of us home.'

'Great.'

'How is Rajeev?'

'He is better; woke up once and I made him talk to his dad.'

'Oh good! Baby, I love you… This…this has been such a terr…terrible night,' Apeksha was crying by now.

'Apeksha… Apeksha…please control yourself darling. I will be home soon. Yes, it's been a terrible night. Love you too, baby! Message me when you get home. I don't have much battery left.'

I fell asleep while watching the news. I woke up to a sunny morning. It was 7 a.m. and the news on television said that the terrorists were still inside the hotel. The commandos had cleared one of the two hotels that had been attacked and the other hotel was still being searched for hidden terrorists. Sporadic gun shots could still be heard which meant that the terrorists were still hiding inside.

I went to Rajeev's room and was relieved to see him awake; having tea and biscuits.

'Hey you are awake. How are you?'

'I am fine. The doctor said I can go but I should get the bandage removed after a day or two. The bullet didn't touch my bone nor did it do any major damage inside.'

'Thank God! Rajeev, I am... I am so sorry. This was my party and I am so sorry.'

'Chill! That is unless you knew about the terrorists,' he joked.

We left the hospital in an ambulance and since my phone now was completely dead, borrowed the driver's phone to inform his parents. I also called Apeksha who was eagerly waiting for me at home with mom and Reena.

We reached Rajeev's building to find his parents waiting downstairs. One could make out from their faces that they had been crying all night.

It was a tearful reunion and as we walked up to the elevator, Rajeev joked, 'Mom, it's all because of Raghu.'

His mom hugged and thanked me for taking care of Rajeev and the family insisted that I eat something before I left for my place.

We continued to watch the news. Planet TV was flashing an update which said that Rajeev Mehra had been shot and was fortunately out of danger. He was, after all, their celebrity journalist.

'Where have these people come from? When will this stop?' Rajeev's mom asked in horror as more news about the attack was shown on television.

'God knows aunty! Just don't step out until all this dies down,' I suggested.

'Raghu, you too are not going anywhere,' she responded in a stern voice.

'My family is already very worried, aunty. They have seen all this so closely and are really shaken up.'

'I can understand, but they are home *na*. They will be more worried if you step out when the whole city is tensed. Talk to them as many times as you want to, but no one goes anywhere from this house till this city is back to normal.'

Rajeev, who was lying on the sofa, supported his mom, 'Yes Raghu, just relax here. Just take some rest. You haven't slept well since yesterday.'

He continued, 'By the way, what it it that you were going to say? You were saying something right…about some confession.'

'Oh my God! You still remember my speech after all this. I don't remember anything about it. We are alive and that itself is shocking.'

'Yes, yes, but what were you going to say?'

'I don't remember… I think… I think I was going to say that I love Bollywood.'

Both of us burst out laughing.

Acknowledgments

It's not possible to take all the names here but I would like to thank each and every person who has contributed in making me what I am today—some have taught me and helped me, some have just been around to give me support, some came in at the right time when I needed their presence.

My mom, in particular, for being the best one in the world and making me the way I am. A lot of people say I am your carbon copy, and if that's true, then I know I am sorted! My wife, Yogita Limaye, gave my life a whole new meaning. Thanks for showing me right from wrong.

I owe my professional life to Rajeev Masand; brick by brick he has built it up for me with or without my knowledge and I value it a lot. Rajdeep Sardesai gave me the opportunities and the platform where I could showcase my work. Thank you for trusting me.

Ajay Mago, publisher of Om Books International, for being positive about my book from the time he heard the story in the first meeting. My editor Shoili Sarkar-Seth for putting in all the hard work and making this book what it is.

Mom often tells me, and it's time I start believing in that: 'Good things happen to good people!'